Calum Kerr is a writer, edito[r, ...based in the] South of England with his w[ife ...(also a writer)], his stepson, Milo, and a menagerie of animals.

He is the Director of National Flash-Fiction Day and his flash-fictions have been published in a wide variety of journals, magazines, e-zines and blogs. He has published two collections, *31* and *Braking Distance*, and has 4 new pamphlets of flash-fictions coming out in early 2013.

More information about him, his writing, and everything else he gets up to can be found at www.calumkerr.co.uk.

Other books by the same author:

31 (2011, Gumbo Press)
Braking Distance (2012, Salt Publishing)

Undead At Heart

by Calum Kerr

GUMBO PRESS

Published by Gumbo Press

First published in Great Britain, 2012, on Kindle by Gumbo Press.
This edition, 2013, Gumbo Press.
www.gumbopress.co.uk

Copyright © 2012 Calum Kerr.

The rights of the above named person to be identified as author of his work has been asserted by him in accordance with the Copyright, Designs and Patents Act, 1988.

All characters in this book are fictitious and any resemblance to real persons, alive or dead, is purely coincidental.

All rights reserved. No parts of this publication may be reproduced or transmitted in any form or by any means, electronic or mechanical, including photocopying, recording or any information retrieval system, without prior permission in writing from the publisher.

This book is sold subject to the condition that shall not, by way of trade or otherwise, be lent, resold, hired or otherwise circulated without publisher's prior written consent in any form of cover or binding other than that in which it is published, and without a similar condition including this condition being imposed on the subsequent purchaser.

ISBN: 978-0-9572713-2-6

For Mum,
*for all your encouragement and support
and your zombie-hunting skills, of course.*

One

Nicola gritted her teeth and gripped the steering wheel hard with her fingers. Some mothers had to cope with endless repeats of the *Rastamouse* theme song, some with The Best of Disney or something equally annoying. For some reason Alyssa, her daughter, was hooked on Bohemian Rhapsody and every time it came to the end of the song she would ask her mother to put it on again.

This was only a short journey, thank God, but they were already on the sixth repeat and, with another ten miles to go in increasingly busy traffic, Nicola calculated that she had at least another five or six to go. Rock legends they might have been, and Freddie might have been the most amazing showman ever to grace a stage. But when Galileo was mentioned for the 65th straight time, she could quite happily have strangled the whole lot of them.

Alyssa's Christmas request was to be taken to go and see the musical, *We Will Rock You*. She knew she would have to bow to her daughter's demands in time, but for the moment she was not engaging with Alyssa's requests in the hope – no, the fervent prayer – that she would forget and find a new obsession. Reading would be good, origami even better. Or maybe bonsai trimming? Nicola smiled to herself, the muscles of her face softening from their rictus for a moment, as she imagined her six year-old daughter trimming a tree which would be almost the same size as her.

The moment didn't last however, as the song reached the end and the voice from the back seat called, 'Again! Again!'

Nicola dropped a weary hand to the stereo and hit the 'back' button to start the track over and resumed her routine grip and grit.

In a more relaxed state, Nicola liked to think that she looked pretty good for her age and certainly nothing like her 34 years. Her naturally-curled hair had now grown long enough to hit her shoulders in a way she liked, the weight of the length pulling the curls into soft loops, rather than the tight rings which they had been for so many years. Its mid-brown shades offset her deeper brown eyes and, she hoped, leant her an air of mystery. However, having caught sight of herself in the mirror on journeys like this, she knew that the tightening of her jaw that could now be caused by just the first few piano notes, rendered her skin too tight and called attention to the underlying sharpness of her features.

She tried to relax, and had a small amount of success, but then the operatic middle came around again and she started to grind her teeth.

She reached down and turned the sound down a little. "Honey?"

"Yes, Mummy?"

"Do you think we could listen to something else for a little while?"

"No, Mummy! Mohebian Bapsody! *Mohebian Bapsody!*"

Wary of a tantrum, Nicola decided it wasn't worth the effort. There was enough danger of tears and stamping when they arrived at the dentist's, so she decided she would have to live with the prog-rock classic just a little while longer.

It was only a routine check-up - at the nearest NHS

dentist which Nicola had been able to find on her return from the States – but suddenly she was hopeful for a filling or an extraction. That would make Alyssa docile enough to let her mum listen to whatever she wanted. Or – oh bliss! – maybe nothing at all.

Of course, this thought was immediately followed by a wave of guilt. How could she possibly wish such a thing on her daughter? But, she reasoned with herself, it was hard bringing up the girl on her own. Never mind the slightly disturbing obsession with a song written over thirty years before the girl was born. Just being six was enough to cause Nicola problems. She blamed Rob, which was, after all, perfectly natural. Bastard. And, she thought, not for the first time, she could also blame him for the musical accompaniment to nearly every car journey she had taken with her daughter in the past two years. It was one of Rob's parting gifts to her. Who plays Queen to a four year old? Who? Rob, that's who. Bastard.

So, if from time to time she weakened and was not the perfect mother but, instead, a weak human being who just wanted a little peace, a little time to herself, then surely that was natural. After all, it wasn't as though she planned to hit Alyssa till one of her teeth came loose, was it? She *wasn't* that bad a mother.

Just having had the thought was enough to make Nicola feel guilty. She blamed Rob again, whispering the word 'Bastard,' quietly under her breath, and turned up the stereo in an attempt to make amends for her evil thoughts. Alyssa didn't know what she had been thinking, of course, but Nicola doubted she'd mind.

Eyes focussed back on the road instead of inward to her problems, Nicola was slightly surprised to see a military helicopter flying low over the road. The trees were thick on either side of this stretch of the A34, presumably to protect the delicate Oxfordshire cows from having to look at all the ugly traffic which sped up and down the road each day.

It was one of those long helicopters with a rotor at both the front and the back. A Sky-hook? Chin-hook? Something like that. It emerged over the tops of the trees on the right like a startled grouse taking flight, crossed low over the road, it's shadow disturbingly large as it trailed over the traffic in front, and then disappeared equally as suddenly behind the treetops on her left.

It seemed strange and incongruous on a nice day like today. She might have been grumbling about the musical accompaniment, but she couldn't complain about the weather or even the view. It was a bright and sunny July day, like the days of the summer holidays that she remembered from before they moved to America. The trees, though thick at the sides of the road, were full and green and reminded her, with a slight pang of not-quite-home sickness, of rural roads she remembered from her time in the States. She made a mental note to come back here in the fall when the leaves would be turning and see how they compared to Maine or Vermont. Her parents had moved to Boston, her father leaving his position at Oxford to take up a Professorship at Harvard, but their holiday home had been in Maine, and holidays had been taken in most of the rest of the top-right corner of the country known as New England. New Hampshire had been her least favourite, probably because most of what she had seen of it had been from the interstate as they drove from Boston to Portland, but she had loved Maine dearly and had hated leaving it. She had to get away from Rob, though, and returning to England seemed her only choice.

Something else to blame Rob for.

Her reminiscences were interrupted by two more of the large helicopters flying almost directly over her car. This time she really did jump in her seat as the loud noise of their passage trailed behind them. Should they really be so low? Was that safe?

Some part of her brain woke up and she remembered that there was a military base nearby. Was it Brize Norton or was that somewhere else. Salisbury Plain wasn't that far away, she was fairly sure. Was that where they were headed?

She drove past a long layby, and noticed that it was filled with green army trucks. There was no sign of the soldiers she would have expected to fill them, and the engines appeared to have been turned off. Nicola felt disquieted.

She found herself staring at the trucks as she drove past them. Finally, as they slipped behind she looked back to the road and saw that she would have to slow as the traffic in front of her had started to bunch up. She watched as her speedometer dropped from 50 to 40 and cursed under her breath. There was a chance that they might now be late, and the dentist was never very accommodating with that kind of thing. If they were she would have to make another appointment, probably at least a month away – partly because they were so busy, but at least partly, she was sure, as a punishment for being late. And then she would have to drive home with Alyssa, un-sedated, calling over and over for her favourite song.

As if this thought was a mental cue, the song once more came to an end and Alyssa called, "Again! Again"

Nicola glanced down, hit the back button on the stereo once more, and looked back up. The huge roar which came from the fields to her left made her give out an involuntary shriek, and then she was straightening her leg on the brake, her whole body going rigid as she tried to get the car to stop in time,

It wasn't the sound of the explosion, nor the stationary traffic which caused this reaction, it was the sight of an articulated lorry flying through the air, the canvas sides of the trailer flapping in flames, heading for the road and the cars in front of her. Despite her foot on the brake, she was still heading for it, and she didn't think they would be able to stop. Her instinct was trying to twist her in her seat to protect Alyssa from the impact, but at the same time her brain tried to work out a way for her to avoid the blow altogether. Could she dodge or weave? Could she duck?

It was with relief that she realised that the truck had been higher than she'd thought when it appeared, like a bizarre echo of the helicopters, over the trees, and was actually heading for the far carriageway. It was bad news for the cars travelling South, especially the sporty silver number which seemed to be on an irresistible collision course with the front of the fiery truck. But she couldn't worry about that now. Adrenaline had flooded her body, leaving her panting, but they had had a lucky escape and she could just travel home – the long way round – and find out about the casualties, and the cause of the explosion, on the news tonight. It was cold and callous, but she had Alyssa to worry about, after all.

She turned away, not wanting to watch as the wagon hit the silver car, and so missed the way that it twisted and rolled as it hit the road, the link between truck and trailer snapping. What she did see, when she looked back, was that the trailer, now free of its anchor, metal frame twisted and canvas still aflame, had flipped back on itself and was going to land right in her path. There was nothing she could do about it and, as Alyssa screamed, Nicola did finally turn in her seat to try, with her slight frame, to stop the tonnes of oncoming metal from killing them both.

Two

"Damn signal." Tony cursed at his Blackberry and shook it, as though that would help. He held it up and pressed the small black rectangle against the roof of his car, glancing between the road and the screen, waiting for some indication that his connection was being re-established.

His car, his pride and joy, his metallic silver Audi TT RS Coupé started to drift out of its lane towards the crash barrier. Tony corrected with a flick of his left hand, his right still holding his phone up by his ear. The car started to swing too far, crossing into the inside lane, and the car he was over-taking sounded its horn, so he pulled back into his lane, gaze still flicking between windscreen and widescreen. "Come on, come on!" he muttered.

Finally, the small icon showing his internet connection popped back onto the screen, and his emails continued to download. He slowly lowered the device, making sure it was still connected, then slid it onto the ledge formed by the steering-wheel housing, and placed both hands on the wheel.

He flicked the stalk for the stereo and jumped forward through the tracks till he found one that he wanted to listen to. He discarded *The Final Countdown* and *You Give Love a Bad Name* in favour of Survivor's *Eye of the Tiger*. His friends laughed at his taste in music. They all listened to bands with little or no musical ability, bands that came from X-Fuctor or Britain's Got No Talent, or bought songs by people they've never heard of 'featuring' other people they'd never heard of. With that great wealth of musical talent on offer, he didn't see how they could scoff because he liked good old fashioned eighties rock. He might only be twenty seven, but that still means he was born, alive and aware in the eighties. Just. And the music of the year he was born seemed perfectly good to him. 1985 had even been immortalised in a song by Bowling for Soup. Which reminded him, he'd listen to Whitesnake next. But first he would rise up to the challenge of his rival.

Anyway, it wasn't his fault. Eighties rock was what his mother had listened to. He'd been weaned to Huey Lewis and his *Power of Love*, taken his first steps to Run DMC's version of Aerosmith's *Walk This Way*. Memories of his first day at school came with a soundtrack of Tears for Fears telling him that *Everybody Wants to Rule the World*. He'd never said it to anyone, and never would for fear that they would laugh at him, but he felt that these songs from his childhood, this body of work that his mother had passed on to him, were his guide in the world. They taught him the life lessons about life that he needed to make himself a success. She had left him a road-map in the form of her music that he could follow once she was gone.

She'd died when he was only fourteen. Breast cancer. A lump was found, but too late. They took the whole thing away, and its partner, but it was too late, it was already moving. From diagnosis to the end was just six weeks, and after he felt like he had blinked and missed it. He had so many things left to say, so many things to ask, but it was too late. Always too late.

But he didn't need her, of course. She'd already passed

on everything that she knew through the songs that she left him. And so he listened, and he learned.

That just left his dad, for what he was worth.

He didn't like music.

A chime from his Blackberry told Tony that his messages had finally finished downloading. He couldn't believe how bad the signal was out here in the country. He didn't mind the long drives that he needed to make for his job, but he did object to having to drive on a road like this. Look at it: all trees and fields. Nothing at all as far as the horizon, when you could see that horizon that is; when it wasn't blocked by more bloody trees. Even if there had been a phone mast in every field, the trees with all their water and sap would suck the signal from the air. He only had one hundred and two new messages, but it had taken nearly ten minutes to download them.

He reached forward to pick up the phone, and started flicking through the messages, scanning the titles. Every so often he'd glance up, make sure he was not heading for anything solid, and perform small course corrections.

Most of them were work-related: adverts for MFD conferences, new products that he should really think about telling his customers about, customers with queries, managers with queries, colleagues with queries. Tony wished he wasn't quite so good at his job. Then he wouldn't get all these bloody queries.

He scrolled past most of them, these weren't the messages he was looking for. Finally, he stopped. 'Looking forward to tonight' was the title. 'redSuse@anymail.com' was the name. It was from a red-headed woman called Susanne Meddler and, he hoped, would tell him where he would be sleeping that night.

He gave himself a little ironic smile as he noticed that the mail immediately after Susanne's was from last night's date, 'gingerKim'. He would read that later, if he had time. Hell, he might even reply. She'd been nice, and a lot of fun, she'd even cooked a decent breakfast. He wouldn't arrange to see her again, he didn't think. If he found himself back in Stoke he was sure there were plenty of other red-headed women who might like a nice night out with a young man who looked as good as he did.

He clicked open Susanne's message and started to read. Yes, she was okay to meet with him tonight. She gave him a time and a place in Portsmouth where they were to meet. She even mentioned that it was close to where she lived. Her final line was a question. She just wanted to make sure that thirty-nine wasn't too old for him. He'd already told her that it wasn't, that it didn't matter what age she was, she was still a beautiful young woman, but he guessed he would have to reassure her. He pressed the button to reply and started tapping away, his thumb moving from key to key, his eyes once more glancing between road and screen.

Of course your not to old. Your the perfect age. You would be beautiful however old you were, but I'm glad I'v met you now as I cant imagine you ever being more beautiful than you are right now. I can't wait to meet you, its going to be wonderful to see you. I just hope you aren't disappointed with me.

love Tony xxx

He hit send and slid the phone back onto his dashboard. For a moment he considered sending an email to Kim. She'd actually been nice and he thought maybe, just maybe, she was worth breaking his rule and seeing her a second time. Either way, she could wait. If he did decide to give her another go then keeping her waiting was definitely the right tactic. And if not, then letting it go cold was always the easiest.

He wondered what all these women thought about him. He knew it was probably cruel of him to woo them so convincingly, work his way into their lives, and then into their beds, and then to disappear. But, hell, that was what internet dating was all about, wasn't it? It was just about people looking to hook up and have a good time. No way did he want to be tied down. He'd seen the effect it had had on his dad when his mum died, and he never wanted to be in that position. And, anyway, he was all over the country all the time, who would want to wait for that? He was being kind really.

His thoughts drifted back to his destination. Not Susanne, she was for later, first there was the client. It was his first University job and he was quite excited and a little nervous. He'd gone straight from school into work at the age of sixteen, so it felt a long time since he'd been in any kind of educational establishment. He tried to remember but didn't think he'd ever actually been in a University. Now here he was, entering like a conquering hero, bringing them the tool which would allow them, yes, to copy, but so much more as well. What he sold weren't photocopiers, they were Multi-Functional Devices. MFDs. You could copy, scan, fax, print, scan to email, email to print, anything you liked. About the only thing they wouldn't do was make you a cup of coffee and he had no doubt that the boffins were working on that. It was the easiest job in the world. These things sold themselves.

He didn't care how educated the people at the University would be, or how many degrees or doctorates they might hold, once they saw the demo machine he had in his back seat they would be climbing over each other to get them installed in their departments. He'd been tasked with getting at least five into the university, but his personal target was twenty. Quietly confident was how he saw that estimate.

His attention was suddenly taken by two dark shapes in the distance. They were large military helicopters, Chinooks, flying over the fields from his left, low over the road, and off behind trees on his right. Just as they were about to disappear from view he saw one of them veer suddenly downwards. There was a huge explosion which made him jerk in his seat. His car was still speeding forward and Tony couldn't understand why his right foot wasn't already on the brake. He shifted it from the accelerator, time seeming to slow, his foot caught in treacle. He started to press on the brake as he saw a truck rise up over the trees from where the helicopter had gone down and his eye tracked it as it flew towards him. It was going to hit him square on.

The sharp braking caused his Blackberry to slide along the dashboard and he reached out to grab it even as the shadow of the truck blotted out the sun.

Three

Nicola opened her door and vomited onto the road. In the distance she could hear the crunching of metal on metal as the cars that were behind her pile-up in a screech of braking. She heard, hell, felt the flames from the truck behind her. More explosions and strange whizzing, cracking noises came from behind the trees, and from the back seat she could hear Alyssa calling her name. None of this seemed to matter. She wiped the back of her hand across her mouth and took the moment to realise that she was still alive.

The trailer had crashed to the road right in front of the car. Nicola had attempted her futile gesture of shielding Alyssa, but had turned back just in time to see the trailer roll onto its top. Both of the sides were aflame, but they were canvas and, even as she looked, they peeled back from the frame. The car jolted as it bumped up onto the upturned roof of the truck, drove through the smoke-filled emptiness and thumped back down onto the road on the other side. She had immediately turned back, pressed down on the brake pedal once more, and slewed the car over to the hard shoulder.

She turned and looked back at the truck. The wooden roof which had provided her with a driving surface was now firmly ablaze and she could barely make out the cars which had screeched to a halt on the other side.

She was alive. She couldn't believe it. She was alive.

'They', she reminded herself. She should be thinking 'they' were alive. She looked back into the car and saw Alyssa, tearful and scared, but whole, and she choked back a sob which nearly turned back into vomiting. The girl saw her looking and held out her arms, calling, "Mummy! Mummy!"

Nicola tried to stand and a wave of nausea and faintness sent her back into her seat. "Just a minute, baby. Just one minute." She lowered her head and took several deep breaths.

When she looked up again she saw the silver car. The one that she had thought must be smashed by the truck. It was parked, its side snuggled up against the burning truck, intact. She could see a figure sitting behind the steering wheel, not moving, and before she knew what she was doing she was sprinting across the road and hurdling the crash barrier.

Four

Tony woke up when she slapped him across the face. He didn't know who she was or what he'd done to her. Hell, he thought, trying to control his confusion, she didn't even have red hair. He didn't have time to work it out before she was grabbing his arm and pulling him from the car. He didn't get far. His seatbelt was still fastened.

She didn't wait for him to come to his senses, but reached past him and hit the release. As she did so her hair brushed against his face and he could smell her shampoo. That worked to wake him as effectively as any smelling salts. He became aware of the passenger side of the car being closer to him than it should be, and the huge wall of metal that filled the window on that side. He remembered what had happened and, even as she was pulling at his arm again, he was levering himself from his seat and pushing up and out. The combined effort sent them both sprawling to the tarmac. She scrambled to her feet, her hand still on his arm, pulling him up and away from his vehicle and towards the relative safety of her own car.

He took two steps with her then stopped. He pulled his arm free and patted his pockets.

"Damn, hold on." He turned back to the car and leant inside.

"What the fuck are you doing?" she screamed at him. She pointed to the buckled front of his car. "There's smoke and shit coming out from under the hood – the... the... dammit!... the bonnet! It's going to explode or something."

He knew this. A quick glance to where she was pointing showed him the increasingly dense cloud which was emanating from the engine. Was that a flicker of flame he saw? But he had to find his Blackberry. The rest could burn, or blow, or whatever the hell it was going to do, but he needed his phone. It was his life.

He scrabbled around in the car and finally saw it lying in the passenger-side foot-well. He dived over and scooped it up from under the bulge of plastic and metal which used to be the door, and pulled back out of the car holding it in the air. "Got it! Let's go!"

He dived past her and starting running towards the crash barrier in the central reservation.

Five

Nicola was wrong-footed as the guy ran past her. Did he really just dive back into a potentially burning car – definitely burning now as bright tongues licked the sides of the hood – to rescue his cell phone? She stood still and watched him run past her, not quite able to believe what she'd seen. He stopped just short of the guard-rail and turned back towards her. "Well, come on then! It's going to blow!" He put a hand on the rail and jumped over.

Watching the crazy man achieve the relative safety of the other lane and head towards her car, and her daughter, brought Nicola back to herself. She ran after him, once more simply hurdling the barriers, landed running and caught up with him as they hurried towards her dark blue people carrier.

"What the fuck were you thinking?" she panted as she reached him. He ignored her, looking back over her shoulder. She turned and watched as the flames took hold and the car started to burn. She had always thought that a car on fire would explode and was slightly disappointed to see nothing more than the fire working its way through the car. The seat where he had been sitting was a torch now, burning brightly despite the midday sun shining down on it. Then the backseat was aflame. And then –

The man grabbed her arm and pulled her behind her car as the flames, which had found their way via the upholstery, finally reached the tank. With a loud bang the back of the car flicked into the air in a shower of metal and fire. A few small pieces of metal bounced off the side of Nicola's car, but the explosion seemed contained and almost docile. Thick clouds of black smoke started rolling down the carriageway towards the stationary cars that had managed to stop before running into the car and truck combination.

As it went up, Nicola heard a scream from inside her car and once more remembered Alyssa. God, what kind of mother was she?! She pushed the man out of the way and yanked open the rear door. Alyssa had already removed the seat-straps and was clambering over to her. She scooped up her daughter and pulled her out of the car, cooing and shushing in her ear, and retreated to the soft verge by the side of the road.

The man followed her and she turned on him, "What the fuck were you thinking? Your car was going up and you had to stop to pick up your phone! What, you going to take a photo of it? A self photo? 'Me and my burning car'? It was nearly you *in* your burning car! You stupid fucking fool!" She could feel tears trying to come, but damn if she was going to cry in front of this asshole.

"Hey! Don't shout at me! I'm not the one who left my child in my car while I went chasing after burning wrecks. I'd have been fine if you left me. I was just about to get out anyway!"

"The fuck you were. You were unconscious. If I hadn't come over there – "

"And if it had gone up when you were 'saving' me? What would have happened to her, eh? Didn't even think about it, did you? Had to be the big hero! God, you Americans, always storming in where you're not needed!"

"I'm not American! And anyway, she was safe inside the car. At least mine wasn't on fire!"

"Well, you sound American!"

Nicola was suddenly aware that they were standing at the side of the road, screaming into each other's faces, Alyssa held in front of her like a shield to protect herself from this crazy Englishman. Alyssa didn't look upset by this shouting match, as she might have expected, but was simply watching them, stunned. Nicola stopped, her mouth open ready to retort, and let it close. She felt all the anger drain from her, taking her energy with it, and took a stumbling step back.

"Yeah, well, I've been away for a while."

"Must have been a long while, you really do sound American." His voice had also dropped down to a normal level.

"Fifteen years, actually, so yeah, a while."

The surrealism of having this conversation while vehicles burned around them and crowds started to gather, moving from their stationary cars to watch the flames, hit her and she let out a laugh. The man smiled in return. She let Alyssa slide from her arms to stand behind her. The girl held onto her hand, but didn't seem to be particularly distressed now she was free of the car, more curious. Her head peered round the man to watch the flames from his car and the truck. Then she looked up and down the road at the people and cars.

"Sorry. Sorry," Nicola said. "I guess I got a fright."

He shrugged. "You and me both."

"Are you okay, though? I thought the truck was going to hit you."

"It nearly did. Turns out my brakes are better than I thought. I skidded and I think I slid sideways into it, or it slid into me. Both, maybe. Whatever. It was a hell of a thump. And then there you were, giving me another one."

"Ha, yeah. Well, you needed it, didn't you?"

He gave a short laugh and nodded. Nicola suddenly realised how young he looked. Poor thing, must be scared, she thought.

She thrust out her hand. "I'm Nicola."

"Tony." He took her hand and shook it, and she he looked her up and down, so consciously that she would have sworn she could feel it. She relaxed her grip and took her hand back, resisting the urge to wipe it on her trousers.

"Well…" she said, looking around them at the scene of devastation. There was no sound of sirens or anything, but she imagined that it was too soon for that.

"Yeah," was his only reply.

They both looked around and nodded for a moment, as though they'd run out of conversation at a cocktail party.

"So," she started again, "What do you think happened?"

"Oh." He seemed startled by the question, but Nicola thought it was quite an obvious one. "Well, there were some helicopters."

"Yes, I saw them. They flew over me. They seemed really low."

He was nodding and already speaking before she finished. "I saw one of them take a dive just the other side of the trees. I guess it crashed on the truck and, I dunno, its fuel tank must have exploded and catapulted it over the trees."

She thought about it for a moment. It sounded reasonable, but – "Would that be enough to throw such a big truck in the air? I mean, your tank exploded and it just lifted the car a bit, didn't throw it over our heads."

"Well, it could have done. I was down to a quarter tank, and a truck's tank is so much bigger. If it was full, and maybe if the helicopter exploded too…" He trailed off and shrugged.

"Well, maybe. But what made it crash in the first place. Did you see anything?"

He shook his head and looked around him again. Again she was reminded of a cocktail party but one where he was growing bored and looking for someone else to talk to. She looked too. More people had gathered from the increasing tail-back. The trailer was still in flames, but they were dying down and she could see people and mangled cars through the frame. The traffic on Tony's side must have been lighter, or more careful, as there wasn't the same scene of wreckage. From the look of it there had just been a few fender-benders.

Finally, after standing in silence, she asked him, "What *is* that noise?" Over the sound of flames she could still hear the strange whizzing and cracking noises from behind the trees.

"Probably ammunition on the helicopters exploding in the heat."

That made sense, she guessed, but she didn't trust this answer either. The noise sounded too electronic for that. It was more like something from movies or a computer games she remembered.

She dismissed it and looked back past the trailer. "It looks like people have been hurt. Should we go and help. It feels strange just standing here."

"We could, but there seem to be plenty of people. We'd only be in the way. Personally I'd just like to get out of here, find some way to get around all this mess and on my way."

"What about your car?"

"It's insured. The police will find it when they turn up, identify it from the chassis number and it'll all get sorted. If I can get to a car rental place, I can get on my way."

"But your things. Aren't you bothered?"

He pointed to the car. "All burned and useless. I'll buy more, no worries. I have everything I need right here." He held up his Blackberry and waved it at her.

She nodded, not really understanding how blasé he could be about all this.

"You're not hurt are you?" he asked.

She shook her head.

"And the sprog's okay?"

"The what?"

"The sprog." He pointed to Alyssa.

"Oh." She looked down at her daughter, who was busy twisting the tassels which hung from the hem of Nicola's short jacket. "Sure, I think so. You're okay, aren't you, honey?"

Alyssa nodded.

"Okay. And your car looks okay, too. A little smoky, but intact."

"Well, yes, I suppose so."

"Excellent." He rubbed his hands together. "So how about you drop me in the nearest town with a car-hire place and we can be on our way."

"What? Just drive away? Leave all this? But shouldn't we stay?"

"What for? What possible good can we do here? Who can we help, tell me that."

She shook her head. Again, he seemed to be making sense but she couldn't help feeling there was more going on here than it appeared.

"I – I guess so." She pushed her hand into her pocket to look for the keys and then realised that not only were they still in the ignition, but the engine had been running all this time.

Tony moved quickly to the passenger door, nodding at her, encouraging her, and she led Alyssa slowly back to the car.

As they climbed in, he was already staring intently at his phone, tapping away on the keys. He said nothing as she settled Alyssa and climbed in herself. She looked around, feeling very wrong to be just leaving the scene of this… well, this whatever it was. But she put the car into 'Drive' and started forward.

They had managed about ten yards when there was another huge explosion, this time from further away behind the trees, accompanied by a strange whirring, whining scream. The engine went dead and all the lights on the dashboard went out.

She heard Tony say, "What the-," and looked over to see he wasn't responding to the failure of the car at all, but was shaking his cell phone. The screen was blank and all his shaking was doing nothing to bring it back.

Six

God, the woman could talk. Okay, so he was grateful that she'd pulled him from the car. He'd really thought he was dead when he saw the truck sailing towards him. Some quick thinking and fast reflexes had saved him, though, and he was sure he would have been awake and out of the car in plenty of time, even without her assistance.

In fact, here she was protesting about him going back in for his Blackberry, but if she hadn't been so damn pushy about him getting out of the car in the first place, he would have remembered it first time round and the extra delay wouldn't have been necessary. Typical bloody American, he didn't care what she said. Her accent was a give-away. Born there, brought up there, it didn't matter. Once the culture got into them it was all fuss and bluster and getting their own way.

At least she had finally seen sense. Okay, something weird was going on here, but he didn't need a flashing neon *billboard* to see that. He just didn't see where that was his business. He had places to be and people – well, person – to see. Really, what good could they do by hanging round here? He hadn't done any first-aid since that one year in Cubs, and she had the sprog to look after. Even if she turned out to be a nurse, what was she going to do, leave the kid at the side of the road while she tended to the wounded? And there was no way he was going to look after the kid. All that screaming and moaning and whining? No thanks.

So, finally, thankfully, he'd convinced her to get into the car, and it looked like he would be getting a useful lift and be back on the road soon as. As much as he could be, with his car in flames, Tony was happy.

Okay, so the demo was going to be less impressive with the MFD currently charring in the backseat of his Audi. And he would have to go shopping for clothes before tonight. He couldn't exactly turn up to his date with Susanne dressed in his work gear and with no over-night bag. But, it could have been worse: at least he had his phone.

As they climbed into the car he started typing. There was a really strong signal just here, which was a blessing, and he needed to let the client know that he might be late, and then he needed to do the same for Susanne. In fact, he would include details of the terrible accident and his miraculous and heroic escape. That might speed things along. Especially when he told her about the woman and her child that he had saved from their car just before it blew up.

He was half-way through his mail to the client when his phone suddenly shut down. He shook it, but nothing happened, so he turned it over and started to prise at the battery. It did this sometimes and he had to take the battery out, put it back, turn it on again, and it would be fine for a while.

He'd just got the battery out when he realised they had drifted to a halt and the woman - Nicola, did she say? – was turning the key in the ignition over and over with no result. He sighed. "What now? Is it out of petrol?"

She turned a sharp gaze on him. "What? No! I filled up

when I set off." She carried on turning the key. Nothing. Just the dry click of the key turning.

"Battery?"

The sharpness when she looked at him had turned to scorn. "No. New last month. It's something else."

Tony's sigh was even louder as he undid his belt, opened the door and stepped from the car. He walked around to the front, flicking his hand at her to open the bonnet. She did so, then got out to join him.

He opened it and started looking around for a loose connection. He didn't really know what he was looking for. Engines had never been an interest of his. But he was sure he would do a better job of finding a loose wire than any woman, especially an ignorant American.

He poked and prodded, taking care not to burn himself on the hot engine or to get dirt on his shirt sleeves. He couldn't find anything. He glanced over at Nicola and saw that she wasn't even looking at the engine, she was staring away from the car to the other carriageway.

She glanced back at him and then pointed. "Look."

In their short journey in the car, they'd moved far enough to draw level with the front of the queue which had formed behind Tony's wrecked car. Some people had left their cars to watch the fire, but many more had initially stayed in safety. These people were now getting out of their cars and opening their bonnets, looking at the engines. Others were standing holding mobile phones in the air and waving them about, much as Tony had been doing just a minute earlier.

He stood up, trying to work out what she was going on about. Okay, it was strange, but he couldn't see what it had to do with them.

"Listen," she said.

He did. He couldn't hear anything, and started to say so.

"Exactly," she cut in over him. "Nothing. No car engine noise, no music playing, no mobile phones ringing. Nothing at all."

He hated to admit it, but she was right.

"What the hell's going on then?" he asked. She seemed to know the answers, so maybe she had this one.

She shook her head. "I'm not sure. It seems like everything has gone dead at the same moment."

She turned to him, but her gaze was drawn up and over his shoulder. Her eyes went wide. He started to turn, but then realised he didn't need to as five fighter jets flew low overhead, their roar trailing behind them. In an instant they were gone, leaving behind a rush of wind and an almighty noise. He watched them head out over the fields, bank sharply and head straight back. He tracked them, raising his hands over his ears to baffle the noise of their passage, and watched as trails of smoke detached themselves from under the wings of the planes and sped away. Moments later there were several explosions in the distant field beyond the place where the helicopter had come down. The noise reached him first, and then the trees bent towards them and a hot, smoky wind rushed over him, making his eyes sting and the air rush from his lungs.

He heard Nicola coughing next to him, and tried to open his eyes to see what was happening.

He eased them open a painful crack and saw that the trees which had screened the field from view were now denuded and on fire. Tiny tinkerbells of flame drifted towards him as the leaves were consumed. Beyond them he could see nothing but fire engulfing the whole landscape.

Tony didn't stop to think. He didn't say a word. He simply turned and ran.

Seven

As Nicola stood, holding Alyssa's hand and looking at the silent cars, she could hear nothing but the crackling of flames from the still-burning truck and the confused voices of deprived motorists, a phrase went through her head: *Electro-magnetic pulse.* It wasn't the kind of thing she would normally know. She was a historian, not a scientist. But Rob had watched enough sci-fi and action movies for her to have picked up the term. Hell, the concept was now so mainstream they even used it in *Ocean's Eleven*. It was what happened when a nuclear bomb went off. It sent out a kind of wave that fried electrical circuitry. Normally it wasn't an issue because the circuitry was fried in other ways too, or so irradiated that no-one would want to use it for thousands of years. That would be one way of getting brain cancer from a cellphone, she mused. Even as she was thinking this, she marvelled at the fact that she was standing in the midst of the insanity that her day had become and was still thinking so clearly.

Tony was asking her what had happened and she was saying she didn't know even as these thoughts were going through her head. It wasn't that she didn't want to tell him, it was more that she had the feeling that he wouldn't hear her if she did. He seemed like a nice enough guy, but – No. Actually, he didn't seem that nice. He reminded her a lot of Rob. He was so caught up himself that he didn't care about anyone else.

He had started ordering her around, telling her to abandon the wounded, telling her to give him a ride to a rental place, and she had simply acquiesced. She had slipped back into the person that Rob had moulded her into without so much as a thought. She hated that it had been so easy for her to give in to him. And even more she hated that it had felt comfortable, like slipping into old shoes.

So, maybe she wouldn't tell him what was going on. Maybe she would keep it to herself and let him work it out if he could. Let's see how capable he was without other people around to look after him.

She turned to him, intending to press *him* for answers, to make *him* take some responsibility for what was happening to them, but her words were stillborn. She watched as an arrow-head of planes swooped low over the trees and passed over their heads in a deafening rush of wind. She felt Alyssa snatch her hand away, needing both of them to cover her ears. Nicola did the same, swivelling to watch the planes flash out over the countryside and then turn and race back towards them. As they passed back over her head she saw rockets strapped to the underside of the wings. Even as she noticed them, flames sparked at their rears and they left the planes behind in the wake of their exhausts. Moments later an almighty explosion rocked the world, causing her to stumble to her knees and clutch at Alyssa who, in turn, clutched at her mother.

A flash of flame dimmed the sun, bared the trees and threw cindered leaves at her on a hot fist of wind. She bowed her head and waited to be burned alive, but there was no further blast. The missiles had impacted far enough away to not kill them, just for them to be caught in the wash. She lifted her head, squinting open her eyes at the heat.

Fall had come early and all the trees were lit in shades of yellow and orange, the black silhouettes of their branches playing host to a raging fire. Behind them the field looked as though it contained a new type of rape which was more than just yellow, it was alive with light. And beyond that? What *was* that?

She was aware, even as she knelt there and held Alyssa tight into her chest that Tony was no longer beside her. She looked round, concerned, and saw him once more vault the central barrier. He continued across the road, down the bank, and disappeared into the trees on the far side. Some of them were starting to smoulder, but they had fared a lot better than the ones on her side.

She turned back and looked through the burning, aware that the heat was growing. She tried to see through the flames and shimmer. There was something there, something moving on the ridge. She could only imagine it was whatever the planes had been shooting at. Whatever it was, it was huge and didn't seem to have been in the least bit bothered by the missile strike.

But she couldn't see it clearly and now the heat was too intense, she could feel her skin tightening as it started to burn. She picked Alyssa up and, more slowly and with extra care for her daughter, she followed Tony.

The crowd on the far side which, like her, had been gaping at the transformation of the landscape, were also starting to back into the relative safety of the trees. She hoisted Alyssa over the rail, climbed over, then picked her daughter up again. As she reached the hard shoulder on the far side she looked back. The trees were starting to fall, bringing burning branches and trunks down onto the carriageway. As she watched, a long branch crashed onto her car. She stood, transfixed, as her people-carrier started to go the same way as Tony's Audi, and might not have moved even when it exploded and the fire started to creep across the road, if someone hadn't taken her arm and started pulling her towards the relative sanctuary of the woods.

She looked round, to find the owner of the hand on her arm. It was a man not that much older than herself, early-forties at a guess, his face covered with the same black streaks that she supposed she was adorned with. He was giving her a confused but soothing smile. "Come on, love," he said, his voice only just audible over the crackling blaze. "Time to get somewhere a little safer."

"But... But... Just what the hell is going on?" she asked him.

He shook his head. "Fuck knows!" He grinned at the look of shock on her face, then pulled on her arm again. "Come on, we better move before the cars start to go up, and the trees on this side of the road too, maybe."

She nodded, glancing back one last time to where her car was now lost in a ball of fire. She felt a moment of guilt, wondering if her wish to be rid of the Queen CD had precipitated all this, then dismissed such a silly thought. With Alyssa held in her arms, head tucked into her mother's neck, Nicola followed her saviour into the cool of the woods.

Eight

Tony ran into the woods, the smooth soles of work shoes slipping on the grass and detritus. As soon he was under the shade of the trees he felt relief from the heat that had been rolling off the burning field. The image of it was still floating before him, imprinted on his retina, and as he ran he careened from trunk to trunk. His earlier care over his shirt was forgotten as moss and dirt created a new pattern over the blue pin-stripe, but his Blackberry was still clutched in his hand. Despite his fear and panic he peered at it every few steps,, focussing on its black screen through the burning haze obscuring his vision, hoping that it would come back to life and somehow transport him from all of this.

Finally, inevitably, he tripped over a root, or a log, or a pine cone, or nothing at all, and sprawled on the ground. His breath was coming in gasps which sounded in his ears like sobs. He tried to calm, to breathe normally, but he no longer seemed have control. He bowed his head and let out a series of loud moans.

He didn't hear her come up behind him, so he squealed and scrabbled away when he felt a hand on his shoulder. The owner of the hand screamed in response, took a step back and fell onto her bottom with a yelp. Tony peered at her in the darkness. It wasn't Nicola, it was someone else. She was young and blonde and slim.

"What?" he asked her, unable to articulate more. "What?!"

She leaned forward, reaching behind to rub where she had landed. "I- I'm sorry," she said, still rubbing and emitting little hisses when she touched a particularly sore part. "I just wanted to see if you were okay; if you'd been hurt. You sounded like you were in pain."

Her voice was soft, but not breathy or girlish, and it calmed him. He felt a sheepish grin form on his lips, only a shadow of his normal charmer's smile, but a step back towards normality nonetheless. "Yeah, sorry, I guess I'm more out of shape than I thought." He saw her quizzical look and explained. "I was wheezing, you know, from running. I wanted to get away before. Well, before whatever happened next."

"What did happen?" she asked.

"I have no fucking idea. There was a helicopter which, I think, blew up a truck. And then all the electrics went down – and, and I still don't know how that happened." He lifted his Blackberry up again, pressing all the buttons and shaking it, trying to find the combination of button-presses and agitation which would resurrect the dead device. "And then fighter jets flew in and blew up a field."

There was silence for a moment and then he laughed. "Now that was a collection of words that I never expected to hear myself say. '*Fighter jets flew in and blew up a field*'!" He laughed louder, ignoring the rise of his gorge and the sting of tears that he could feel accompanying it. The girl started to laugh too, but a little more uncertainly. Tony just laughed louder. "They must really *hate* the countryside!"

His laughter was howling now, and he was aware it was going on too long, but he couldn't stop it. Eventually it caught in his tightening throat and he started coughing.

The girl came to his side again, slapping his back, and when he could breathe properly again, the laughter had gone and taken the urge to cry or vomit away with it.

He looked up at her and smiled, aware that his eyes were watering, but not caring as these were from coughing, certainly not crying. He was about to ask her name when other people started to appear through the trees. They were walking, rather than running, and some of them had started to talk to each other, comparing their experiences, trying to work out what was going on. Some of them spotted Tony and the girl and a group formed around them. It seemed, for the moment, that everyone felt comfortable being this far inside the forest, and many of them sat down on the ground until it started to look like some bizarre family outing.

Although they were all talking about what they had just seen, no consensus could be formed on what was happening. The subject of the electrics was mentioned and Tony heard a voice say, "I think it was an EMP: an electromagnetic pulse." He looked up to see who it was who had silenced the group, and saw Nicola. "It's one of the side-effects of a nuclear bomb." Tony heard somebody gasp at this, and saw Nicola turn her head to look at the culprit like a teacher with an unruly student. "It *wasn't* a nuclear bomb, of course, or we'd all be dead. But that's where they're usually found. It knocks out all the electrical equipment in the vicinity. So no cars will work, no phones, no radios, nothing."

Everyone was silent for a moment after this, absorbing the information. Many people slipped phones which they had been holding, or fiddling with back into their pockets or bags. Tony held onto his. He wasn't quite ready to give up on it yet. After all, maybe this American woman was wrong. Maybe it just needed a few minutes rest.

"Can they do that sort of thing?" a man at the edge of the circle asked Nicola.

She shrugged, and it was only then that Tony realised that the dark shape in her arms was her daughter. "I thought it was just a thing on movies, something good to move along the plot. They used it in *Ocean's Eleven*. But, obviously, it looks like somebody can."

"Somebody? Who? Are we being attacked?" asked another voice, and then everyone seemed to be speaking at once.

"Is it the Russians?"

"The Chinese?"

"Aliens?"

A few people laughed at this last one, but again Nicola shrugged. "Who knows? Could be."

"Yeah, right!" Tony was surprised that this last voice was his. "Aliens are going to come down and attack rural Oxfordshire. They really hate wheat and barley. No, I know, the colour of oilseed rape offends their eyes so they have come to wipe it off the earth!"

"Oh, shut up," a man nearby told him, weariness in his voice. "There's no need for that!"

"Isn't there? Well, who died and made her the leader?" Tony was on his feet, pointing his phone at Nicola as though brandishing a weapon.

Nicola looked at him blankly. "Leader of what?"

"Of... of..." Tony looked around, trying to work out what he had meant, but it seemed to slip away from him. He sank back down onto the ground, and continued pressing the buttons of his phone where he held it in his lap. The blonde girl, who was still next to him, gave him a reassuring pat on the knee.

The man who had told Tony to shut up, then turned to Nicola. "So, he asked her. What do we do now?"

Nine

Nicola gaped. Why was he asking her that? Hell, why was he asking her anything?

She had just pointed out to Tony that there was nothing to be a leader of. They were just a band of people who had been caught up in a terrible accident and were taking shelter in the woods to escape a fire. Soon enough there would be police and ambulances and fire engines and people to tell them where to go, what to do, and who to claim from for their insurance. She wasn't the leader of anything, as there wasn't anything to be a leader of.

Ah yes, said a voice in her head, *but what about the fighter jets. This isn't just an accident. Those were military planes firing rockets at something. Who says anyone's coming? Who says there's anyone out there to come? All bets are off, I reckon.*

It was a voice best ignored, she decided. She pulled her mouth closed and took a long breath through her nose. "I have no idea," she finally replied. "I know no more about this situation that any of you. What do *you* think we should do?"

The man looked back at her and said nothing. She could see that his inner voice was relaying the same information to him as hers had, and he no more wanted to appoint himself the decision maker than she did.

Nicola had a sinking feeling though. She remembered doing jury service a few years ago in Boston. The first job of the jury had been to choose a foreman, and she had determinedly not volunteered. As she might have expected, it was the most loud-mouthed and most reactionary of the group, a large guy called Bob, who wore red suspenders over a blue plaid shirt, who had asked for the job. That had been fine by her. She just hadn't wanted to be responsible for standing up and delivering a verdict in full view of the plaintiff and the defendant.

But it hadn't been that simple. Once they'd heard the case, a disturbing one about a man who was 'uncle' to a couple of mid-teen girls and was accused of behaving 'irresponsibly', they'd retired to the jury room to discuss it. She tried her best to just sit and listen, but the foreman kept quoting evidence incorrectly and leading people to conclusions that just weren't borne out by the evidence. Eventually, she had started to interject, and then a little more. By the time a verdict was reached she was aware that she had managed to lead them to *her* conclusion, and one or two had asked her, in the breaks, why *she* wasn't the foreman.

It wasn't that she had wanted to take control, it was just that she couldn't just sit back and let others let their stupidity or their prejudices talk for them. She just had to speak up.

She could feel that same thing creeping over her now, especially as Tony looked up from his phone and said. "Well, I think we should just stay here."

She bit her tongue and waited. She had no desire to claim any kind of leadership role here, especially when one was already being tendered towards her.

"Something's going on. We know that," Tony continued. "But the fire's on the other side of that nice wide road, and it surely can't be too long before police and ambulances and all that turn up. After all, that's a major road out there, blocked with our cars. I think we stay in here where it's cool, and dark, and not on fire, and we take turns to pop back and look out for the authorities. Then, when they turn up, we can just head out to them." He nodded and looked around. Nicola could tell from his expression that he was waiting for everyone to applaud or something.

Before she said anything she checked inside for any sense of jealousy. She didn't want to speak up. God knows she had no desire to appoint herself as a leader of this group of people. She had enough to look after with the – now-sleeping – bundle in her arms that was Alyssa. But she couldn't sit back and let these people listen to the cowardly crap that Tony was talking.

"No, you're wrong." Her voice came out as little more than a whisper, but a few heads turned to face her.

She tried again. "You're wrong." Her voice was louder this time and she felt it carry, turning every head towards her this time. "If we stay here, I think there's every chance that we might just die."

Ten

"Die? Die! What the fuck are you talking about?" Tony wasn't sure why he was getting so agitated by Nicola, but he couldn't stop himself from arguing. "There's been an accident, sure. And something weird is going on. But, come on, this isn't one of your blockbuster movies with the world coming to an end. It'll be sorted soon and then they'll come and help us."

One or two people made noises of agreement, but many more were looking at him with consternation, confusion, or downright hostility on their faces. He looked around, hoping that common sense would win out, but as he saw the looks on their faces, he started to lose hope. He felt the blonde girl give his leg a reassuring squeeze.

Nicola hadn't taken her eyes off him. She seemed to be holding back from whatever it was she wanted to say. They were facing each other across about twenty yards of forest, with thirty or so other people arrayed around and between them, but for a moment it seemed as though it was just the two of them. Finally, she broke. "Maybe. Maybe not. Maybe it's a training exercise gone wrong and soon there will be flashing blue lights and mugs of tea. But, look at what just happened. A bunch of fighter jets just fired missiles over your head into an ordinary field. This isn't Iraq or Afghanistan. This is England. If they're doing that, then something is going on. And even if it's going on here and nowhere else, it seems to me that the 'authorities' are far too busy to bother with us. We need to move away before the fire spreads over to this side of the road. Or before whatever they're firing missiles at moves over here and they feel the need to fire missiles in this direction."

Oh God, thought Tony, *she's making a bloody speech!* "You said it yourself. Something's going on here, and we don't know what it is. But if we don't take some control, take some responsibility for ourselves, then we have no-one to blame if anything happens to us."

People were making more noises of agreement, and there was a lot of nodding. Tony wanted to disagree, but couldn't find the words, just a stubborn seething.

"So, if we're going to do something. I think we just head away from whatever's happening over there." She pointed back towards the road." And we find somewhere where we can be safe. If we move far enough maybe we can find somewhere with a working phone, or at least a radio or television. Something which might tell us what to do, or what the hell's going on."

All faces were looking at Nicola now. Although nobody was moving, he could feel them drawing away from him. He was left sitting alone in his pool of shadow. Then Nicola turned from where she had been addressing the group, and looked straight at him. "What do you think?"

Tony was taken aback. He hadn't expected her to throw it back at him like that. He said nothing for a moment, and then rose to his feet, looking around at the faces that were now all pointing at him.

"I'm staying," he said. "This is not a Hollywood movie where the creeping terror is going to come and attack us. This is real life. And, this is England. Leave if you want to, and ten minutes after you've gone, when the accumulated weight of the emergency services arrive, I'll make sure to tell them where you've gone. If you've not got lost in the woods, or fallen off a cliff, or whatever, I'm sure they'll find you soon. Me, I'm going to wait, and I'd be happy to have any of you with me."

He nodded at Nicola as if to say: your turn. He looked assured and confident but his mind was reeling. This was all happening too quickly. One minute he was driving along thinking of Susanne, the next he found himself forming a splinter group of people stranded by an accident. He wanted to say this. He wanted to admit that he was scared and didn't know what he was doing. He wanted someone to just tell him what the fuck was going on. But instead he set his face against this woman that he didn't know from Eve, and took his stand.

She nodded back at him. "Fine. That's your right. But I'm going." She didn't make the same invitation to the others that he had, but she didn't need to. She just started walking across the forest floor towards him. She smiled as she reached him then carried on walking, deeper into the woods. After a beat of time, most of the rest of the crowd followed her. Tony turned and watched and slowly, inexorably, they disappeared from his view.

He turned back and now there were four of them: the blonde girl who seemed to have attached herself to him, and a middle-aged couple dressed in fancy clothes which looked completely out of place amongst the trees. The woman smiled an embarrassed smile at him as he looked at her bright blue dress, large matching hat, and sparkly high-heeled shoes. "We were on our way to a wedding."

Eleven

Sam sat and watched the others walk away. She started to stand, but then they were all around her and it would feel weird to be rising to her feet surrounded by all these people, so she stayed where she was. It felt weird anyway, sitting there while they loomed over her, but her man was standing over her and she felt safe. He said nothing, just watched them walk away, but she could tell that he felt sad for them. They had chosen to listen to the panicking woman who wanted them all to run away, rather than listen to his sensible argument. Of course there would be people coming to help them. Of course the police and ambulances would be here soon. Of course they'd be okay.

The clearing emptied and she looked up at him. He was just staring after them, watching them leave. He looked around and spoke to the other sensible couple who had decided to stay. Then he looked down to her and offered his hand to help her to her feet. She rose from the ground and stood next to him, looking up at him, and waited to find out what his plan was now.

It wasn't the first time she'd been sent to the other store to pick something up. One branch in Winchester and one in Oxford meant they were close enough to swap stock when necessary without having to use a courier company. But they were also far enough apart that it was a full afternoon's trip. Of course, stopping for a latte and a cupcake with Sandra always made it a slightly longer journey. That was how she'd happened to be driving back from Oxford when she'd seen the truck fall out of the sky in front of her. As always she'd been leaving a sensible distance in front of her. It was, after all, her boss, Ryan's car, and there was no way she wanted to damage it in any way. She'd pulled up about a hundred yards from the accident and watched that loud American woman rescue the man from the car. She watched them run from the burning car and then set off to leave. She was disappointed when she saw him get into the car with her. She couldn't quite understand how they could have known each other, but she guessed it was his lucky day. Now, having seen them arguing, she guessed that they hadn't known each other at all. She presumed that that woman had forced him into her car. She wanted to run away and needed someone to protect her, Sam guessed.

When the cars had all cut out, he'd taken his chance and run away from the crazy bitch, and Sam had followed. She was aware that the trees at the side of the road had burst into flames, but was more intent on following him.

She caught up with him in the woods, where for a moment he seemed to be crying. He explained that he was just breathing heavily from being out of shape. She could understand that, but he didn't look out of shape to her. He looked just fine.

"I'm Sam. Samantha," she said once she was standing again.

"Tony," he said, his eyes already wandering away from her to look around the woods. She loved the way he was taking control of the situation. She wanted to ask him what he thought was happening. She was sure he knew but just didn't want to show off in front of everyone else. She did know that he was making a plan, however, and didn't want to interrupt, so she left him to his important thoughts and went over to talk to the other couple who had been sensible enough to stay.

She introduced herself to Bob and Janet. They had been on their way to Janet's niece's wedding. "It's only a few miles. I said to Bob that we should take the back road, go through the nice countryside. I said that if we went onto the main road all that would happen is that there would be a traffic jam and we'd get stuck. And I was right, wasn't I, Bob?" Bob nodded. "Not that I knew it would be anything like this. Trucks falling on us from the sky? Fighter planes bombing us? The car cutting out on us? Having to run for our lives into the woods? I mean, what on Earth is going on? And how are we going to get to Aimee's wedding now? If our car won't go and the road is blocked, what exactly are we meant to do? And that woman was all very well, but I said to Bob when she was talking, I said 'Bob, it's all very well panicking and making a fuss, but I think we should do like the nice man says and stay and wait for the police. Maybe,' I said to Bob. 'Maybe they'll even give us a lift to Aimee's wedding – what with it being a special day and everything – and if they need to take a statement, maybe we can come in and make it later.'"

Samantha smiled politely at this barrage of information. Working in a very upmarket dress shop she was used to women who would come in and talk at her without really expecting any response.

"I just hope that being here in these woods hasn't ruined

my shoes. After all it's pretty muddy. I mean, I know the weather's been nice and it's been dry for the last two weeks. Bob and I have been able to eat out every evening, haven't we, Bob?" Bob nodded again. "It's been lovely because we only got it redone last year, and this year all the flowers have really taken off. I mean, they were nice last year, but everything was so new that it needed a year to bed in." She paused, and for the first time as far as Sam could tell, Janet took a breath. "Anyway… It's been so nice, and I've got a lovely tan, but this ground is so soft my heels are sliding in and I'm worried they're going to be ruined for the wedding. Do you think they are going to be very much longer?"

Sam was taken surprise, not by the nature of the question, but by the fact that there was a question at all. She said nothing for a moment, except an indeterminate, 'Erm…" and then there was a huge blast of wind and an almighty thump which shook the ground and knocked her over backwards. She slid down into the depression left by the roots of a fallen tree, and rolled over onto her face. She heard a loud crash and scrabbled round onto her knees, wiping her hair from her face even as she wiped mud onto her skin. She peered up to where she had been standing and was faced with a large, unidentifiable scramble of metal. It was streaming smoke, and seemed composed solely of sharp and charred edges.

Sam stumbled to her feet, and then screamed as she saw a very muddy, but instantly recognisable pair of shiny, blue high-heels sticking from under the wreckage. A pair of slightly thick ankles still emerged from the shoes and disappeared, amongst a spatter of blood, under the metal. Of Bob, there was no sign. She fell to her knees and screamed and screamed until Tony came over and pulled her away. She buried her head in his chest and continued to scream as he attempted to coax her into movement. In the end he gave up, scooped her into his arms, and staggered off into the forest.

Twelve

Stan looked over at Dave and raised his eyebrows. Once he had his brother's attention, he cocked his head in the direction of the woman who had introduced herself as Nicola.

Once they had gone far enough to be out of sight of the clearing where they had left that incredibly stubborn guy and his 'followers' she had stopped to tell them her name and that she had no intention of being their leader, she just thought they should get away. Once they had, she told them, someone else who knew what they were doing could take over.

Even as she said it, though, Stan could feel everyone hitching their attention and their hopes to her. She may not know it, but she had something about her which made everyone want to trust and follow her. She was their leader, simply because she was, whether she wanted the job or not.

Dave looked back and nodded. He knew what Stan was thinking. The girl might be carrying a child in her arms, and this might be completely the wrong time to be thinking such things, but she was seriously hot. Stan had been the one to disagree most defiantly with the crazy guy, and also the one who had asked Nicola what she thought they should do. When she opened up with the comment about the EMP, he'd known that whatever her background, wherever she came from, her brain was still working in the midst of everyone else's panic. If nothing else, she would keep her head and, Stan hoped, that would help him to hold onto his.

Brains and beauty. This could be Stan's chance for a real catch. If following her and doing what she said was the way to charm her, then he was more than willing to do that.

They carried on through the woods, making decent time. He didn't know where she was leading them, but it seemed that she just wanted to put as much distance as possible between them and the field of fire. It was not so much a case of where they were going to. The important word was 'away'.

A rattling thump shook the ground and caused Stan to stumble. Dave caught his arm and kept him from falling on his face and then the two of them turned to each side, helping up those who hadn't been so lucky. Small pieces of burning metal and other debris started to rain through the canopy. Some dropped onto the leafy ground, starting smouldering fires. One piece landed on Stan's shoulder, burning straight through to his skin. He let out a yelp and brushed at it, his hand singeing in the same movement and coming away with black char marks and blood from his shoulder.

Other people cried out as smaller and larger pieces struck them, and the group broke into a ragged run, trying to outdistance this burning rain.

An older woman stumbled in front of Stan and he simply caught her round the waist like a rugby receiver as he headed past, keeping her on her feet and helping her on her way, thanking the years of ploughing his way up the sport's field on a Sunday morning. He was aware of Dave on his other side, the two of them forming a team of assistance as they made their way through the jostling, fearful crowd.

Finally the downpour ceased and they slowed again as they realised the bombardment had stopped. People turned to one another, stranger to stranger and inspected burns and wounds. It seemed that they had escaped largely unscathed, with most injuries consisting of small burns which didn't seem too bad. One or two people held handkerchiefs or pieces of torn clothing over larger injuries, but everyone seemed to be able to carry on.

It was only at this point that Stan noticed that their group contained no children apart from the girl that Nicola had been carrying. He guessed it was partly because it was the middle of a school day, but maybe they'd also not made it away from the road – either through a misguided belief that it was safer to stay, or because with children to slow them down they hadn't made it to their impromptu gathering in the woods. Whatever it was, Stan wasn't going to worry about children who weren't even there, he just thought it was interesting.

He wondered what sort of airburst had caused the rain of burning metal and wondered if one of the jets they'd seen previously had exploded for some reason. There was no way of knowing, unless he went back to search for larger debris; something he was definitely *not* going to do. He was just curious. With each new event, each new catastrophe, he grew more and more confused about just what was going on.

As though his thoughts about children had cast a spell, he noticed that Nicola's girl was awake and now standing next to her. The girl was unhurt by the falling fire, but her mother was cradling her upper arm. She had torn a strip off the bottom of her t-shirt and was attempting to wrap and tie it with one hand. Stan stepped over and took the strip from her, tying it over a shallow burn which was weeping ever so slightly.

He smiled at her as she winced. "Don't worry, love, we'll find somewhere soon where you can wash that and put some cream on it."

She returned a weak smile. "Well, I hope so. After all, somehow I seem to have become the leader of this gang and I guess I'm responsible if we don't." Stan thought that the smile lit up her face, but he could see signs of stress and pressure which were undoubtedly not new, but he imagined that today wasn't helping matters much.

"Don't worry. This is England, not America. You can't go very far without finding another town, or at least a farmhouse, hotel or pub. Hell, I'm surprised these woods have gone on as long as they have. I thought the only trees left in this country were being kept in nature reserves."

She nodded, partly in agreement, partly acknowledging his attempt to make her feel better. "That's true, we're not exactly out in the wilds, are we?" Her smile was more genuine this time and Stan thought he might be making a little break-through with her.

"I'm Stan, by the way." He held out his hand.

She took it and shook it. "I know, I remember." *Nice!* thought Stan. "I'm Nicola." She smiled again. "But I guess I've been loud-mouthed and annoyingly assertive enough for you to remember that too."

Stan was about to respond with something complimentary which would let her know that she didn't need to be so hard on herself, when Dave walked up and ruined the moment, as usual.

"Stan? Erm… Nicola? I think we've found somewhere." He pointed over to the left and Stan saw the edge of a path which seemed to have simply appeared in the woods. Small posts with swags of rope linking them headed off into the undergrowth and a few of the group were already milling around a sign at the end. Dave led the three of them over, and Stan was impressed to see how the group parted to let Nicola through. He moved in behind her, stealing some of her authority by his proximity to her, and so was able to see the sign. It was a rustic board with an arrow pointing along the path. It said 'Downside Outdoor Pursuits Centre.'

Thirteen

Despite being able to do forty wrist curls, with 15 kilos, three times a week at the gym, Tony was only able to manage about twenty yards over the uneven ground before he needed to set Sam back onto her feet. The large lump of twisted metal had been followed by a rain of smaller pieces, some of which had fallen heavily into the undergrowth sending up small streamers of dark smoke. Others had drifted down around him, sparks in the darkness, like being inside the descending cloud from a firework. One had lit on his hand, like a hot needle digging into his flesh, and for a moment he nearly dropped the girl, but he'd managed a few more steps as the rain came to an end.

Finally, unable to go any further with his burden he let her slide from his arms and was grateful to see that she was able to stand now. She had stopped screaming when he picked her up, but she was still making small whimpering noises. He tried rubbing her shoulder and making shushing noises, but he wasn't sure that he was really having any effect.

He'd never been good with crying women. When they started it was usually his cue to leave. And, if he could manage it, the crying would only happen when he was long gone. Or so he assumed. He had so little contact with the women he saw, that he could only imagine their heartbreak and sobbing when they realised he was never coming back, and that his initial promises had all been false.

Sam slowly came back to reality, reaching into the small handbag which Tony only now noticed she had been clutching, for a tissue to dry her eyes. She wiped them, and her face, and blew her nose. Her hand dipped back into her bag, disappearing the tissue, and came out with an even smaller bag. From that she extracted a compact mirror, which she used to inspect her face. Then, with a tut, she started to pull out small items of makeup with which she started to reconstruct the mask which had been disturbed by her tears.

Tony stood and watched her, wanting to tell her to hurry up. The urge to get away from whatever cataclysm they had been caught up in had finally taken him over and he wished he had gone with the others. At least they would have had someone who could have taken care of Sam for him. He'd known her for such a short while but was already resenting the responsibility she represented. He didn't know the words, however, to ask her to put her makeup away and come with him away from the zone of fallout, so he simply watched her.

With each dab of foundation and each sweep of a brush she seemed to grow more composed, and he started to reason that letting her have this time to rebuild her façade was probably the best answer to her distress. At least, he thought, *as long as nothing else blows up while we're standing here.*

Finally she seemed satisfied with her repair job. She put her tools back into their pouch, and the pouch back into her bag, and turned to him. He could still see the redness around her eyes, but he had to admit she looked a lot better. In fact, she looked a lot more than simply 'better'. She might not have red hair, but Tony was suddenly glad to be responsible for her. This whole event might not turn out to be a complete washout after all.

"I'm so sorry, Tony. I know I need to keep my head if we're going to be okay, but it was just such a shock. I mean, I was talking to them and then... then..."

Tony could see she was on the edge of tears again, and moved to head them off. "I know. Terrible shock. Terrible business all round. I don't know what the world's coming to. But what else were you going to do? Terrible shock. Terrible business. But you're okay now. I'm okay. *We're* okay. Still, I think, maybe, the others were right. Whatever's going on over there," he pointed in the direction in which he thought the road lay, though he honestly was no longer sure, "is obviously still going on and might even be spreading. We need to get somewhere safe, somewhere where we can contact the authorities and get help. I think we should see if we can catch up to them."

Sam took all this in, and Tony was pleased to see the way her composure came back as he spoke. Maybe this responsibility lark was not as hard as it was cracked up to be.

"You're right, Tony. So right. I'm so glad I stayed with you."

Tony nodded, and smiled, looked around them and then, taking her hand, led her off into the woods.

Fourteen

The path very quickly turned into a trail which led through woods which became more and more manicured as they progressed. It was hemmed in on both sides by more of the stake and rope fences, causing them to walk side by side. Nicola found herself at the front, of course, with Alyssa at her side. The girl seemed remarkably unaffected by the day, although she had been quieter than usual. She looked around her as they walked, seemingly enjoying this unscheduled trip into the countryside, and Nicola wondered how much of what had happened she was actually taking in.

Stan and his friend, who she seemed to think was called Dave, and actually might be his brother now she thought about it, walked behind her. Stan seemed to have decided to be her bodyguard, or consort, or something, since he had first guided her entrance to the forest. Behind them the rest of the group had paired up. Some were nursing wounds from the falling debris, but each of these had found someone to help them, to keep pressure on wounds or help them walk where the injury was to feet or legs. It was a model of altruism that, to be honest, she didn't expect. Not in England, anyway. She had encountered some nice people, sure, people who would willingly help each other for no personal gain. But she had also met many selfish people who just wanted to keep their heads down and wait for someone else to take responsibility. People like Tony. She hadn't been able to believe the show he'd put on. What was he hoping to prove? What was he hoping to achieve? All he'd managed to do in the end was convince three other people to risk their lives with him. She knew he was scared, but where was the basic human desire to run away. Only an Englishman, she thought, even as she cringed at her mental voice sounding like a typical American.

Since she'd come back she'd done her best to fit in. She knew how people in this country thought of Americans and, hell, she agreed with most of them. It didn't help that Rob had embodied all of those things that people hated most about Americans. He was loud, brash, opinionated, and ignorant of anything outside his corner of the world. His concession to exoticism and worldly-wisdom was to have married a once-English woman. She wasn't sure which she hated most: that she had been a trophy wife, or that it had taken her six years to realise it.

On her return she had tried to fit back into English society, regain the accent she had worked so hard to lose at fourteen, when she had found herself as the 'foreign' girl in her class, tried to remember what it was to be quiet, and to keep her opinions to herself, and to complain only about the weather. She had tried, but somehow the second half of her life was proving much harder to shed than the first.

Still, she reflected, if it was the dreaded influence of Americanisation – an international infection which she was accused of spreading by anyone with more than one drink in them – that had led to the cooperation between this random group of strangers, then she was finally pleased to have been a carrier of the virus.

As the path wound through the woods, occasional breaks in the ropes led to activity areas: a platform with a zip-wire running from it, a rope net slung from a tree, a rickety bridge over a large mud puddle. But something was wrong. The zip wire sagged in the middle almost to the ground, ready to guide anyone stupid enough to use it straight into the floor. The net had come loose at one corner and hung down like a malevolently winking eye. Slats had fallen from the bridge giving it a gap-toothed smile. It had seemed such a find: an Outdoors Centre would be well-stocked with first aid materials, and who knew, they might be far enough away from the EMP for working phones or at least a radio. Now Nicola was starting to realise that what they would find would be an empty building, its sign hanging loose, and no help to be found.

At least, she thought, if it was empty and abandoned they could break in and find shelter while they did what they could with the injuries and protect themselves from any more falling debris. If they were lucky there might be some abandoned supplies. Even some old sheets would help as makeshift bandages.

They weren't lucky.

They rounded the final corner into a wide clearing and Nicola discovered that even her carefully studied, bleak outlook had been hopelessly optimistic. At some point there had been a fire which had reduced the Centre to a few blackened shards of metal framing: rotted fingers grasping at the sky; and a pile of ashes and molten glass. Small streams of smoke emerging from leaves which had piled in the debris of the buildings showed that the rain of burning that they had endured in the forest had reached at least this far, the clearing providing no barrier to the sky.

Nicola took only a few steps into the clearing and the group formed into a semicircle behind her, lining the boundary between trees and space. A low moan came from a few who had not realised the significance of the broken-down activity areas.

Nicola thought that she should probably say something to them. These people had followed her, and she had led them away from their original direction in the hope of finding help at this Centre. Although it wasn't her fault, she felt that she had in some way let them down.

Before she could say anything, however, she heard Stan clear his throat. "Ah well, it was worth a try." His voice was conversational but loud enough to reach them all. "At least we've found a road."

Nicola turned in surprise and saw him pointing past the burned wreckage of the buildings which had captured her vision, to where a tarmacked road, covered by the fallen leaves and branches of who knew how many years, led away from what would once have been the car park for the Centre.

Her heart lifted. She might not have found help, but she had helped them find a route that might lead them to somewhere better. Where there was a road, there would be – eventually – civilisation.

She set off to circle the shell of the Centre, but was pulled up short by Alyssa who still held her hand, but refused to move. Nicola looked down at her daughter and saw her pointing above the trees on the far side of the clearing. Following the pointing finger with her gaze, Nicola could see three shapes in the sky. They were vaguely triangular, but these were no jets. They were hovering like helicopters, but there were no rotors. As she watched, they zigged and zagged from side to side, contrails of missiles fired from the ground passing between them, and Nicola realised they were hovering somewhere over the burning field from which they'd fled.

From their bases, thick green streams of light shot out, parallel to the paths of the missiles. A few moments after the appearance of the beams, Nicola could hear a singing, whining noise which was accompanied by a rumbling, roaring, crumbling noise like a distant rock-fall. The three UFOs started to move closer, and so did the noise. If they kept on in a straight line it wouldn't be very long before the beams, and the steadily loudening noise, would arrive at the clearing in which they were standing.

Once more she scooped Alyssa into her arms, turned to face all the people who were still staring at the apparitions in the sky, and screamed, "*Run!*"

Fifteen

Tony hated the countryside. He always had. He'd been brought up in North Manchester where grass was for parks and trees were the things which they periodically planted on the edges of pavements and left to die. He'd never seen the attraction of walking the hills or wandering by the sides of rivers. He was a creature of the city-centre; of clubs and pubs, shops and restaurants, paving stones and tarmac. He wasn't sure he'd ever really thought about it, but he hadn't known that such places as this really existed. This was not the kind of woods that you saw on television with rosy-cheeked couples walking hand in hand, their over-sized dog bounding around them looking for sheep to worry. There were no paths in this forest, just trees and fallen leaves, mud and stone and moss. His city shoes slid on the slickness under foot, a crust of mud forming around the leather sole. Sam stumbled after him, the heels of her shoes, admittedly shorter than they might have been, either sinking into the soft ground, or skittering on stone. She hung onto his arm and he half-guided, half-carried her through the dimness.

He kept expecting to come across some kind of path or clearing, but these woods seemed entirely unmanaged and untouched by human hand. He wondered how long it had been since anyone had walked between these trees, or even if they ever had. Maybe this was primordial forest that had never known man's presence before.

This thought was cut short when they passed around another of the impenetrable stands of trees which blocked their way, to see that the trees ended only a hundred yards in front of them. The woods thinned allowing sunlight to light the ground, and then there was grass visible beyond.

As they walked towards this oasis of light the leaf-litter became more sparse and the ground grew more solid underfoot, making the going easier and allowing them to move faster. A few yards from the end of the shade, Tony saw a picnic bench sitting on the grass in the sunlight. For a moment he wondered if it was a mirage, a drowning man spying a pool of water with its attendant date trees. But it never wavered, and as they emerged finally into the light he saw that it was not isolated. Beyond the bench were four, five, six, ten, twelve more. They led in a scattering to a large brick building with a glass conservatory. And then Tony saw the sign at the front which announced this was The Hare and Hounds. They'd found a pub, and for a moment Tony considered believing in God.

Now onto the soft grass, Sam paused to remove her shoes, and they half-ran over the grounds to the building. There were no lights showing from inside, but there were half a dozen cars parked outside, and the doors and windows were open. As they reached the car park Sam stopped again to put her shoes back on. Tony waited impatiently, and then as soon as she had them back on, set off again, with her trailing him. He neared the open doors of the conservatory and heard voices inside. At last! People! Someone who could help him.

They walked into the bright conservatory and looked around. There was no-one in the room in which they found themselves, though there were some half-eaten meals grown cold on one of the tables near the window. The voices were coming from deeper inside, in the gloom of the pub proper. Probably gathered at the bar, Tony thought, and led Sam through.

The talking stopped as everyone watched the newcomers walk in.

A large dark-haired man and a much smaller, rounded blonde woman were standing behind the bar. In front of it, his hand raised, finger accusing, in the middle of making a serious point was an older man with a shrew-faced woman next to him. Beyond them, perched at the bar were a young couple. She was holding a babe in arms, cooing to it. Two men in builder's garb were beyond them, and then finally were what looked like the chef and the waitress for the pub's restaurant.

Tony raised his hand at all the eyes staring at him. "Erm… hello?"

"Ah good, someone who is bound to agree with me," said the angry man at the bar. The woman Tony presumed was his wife nodded, while the others rolled their eyes. The man who appeared to be the landlord simply sighed.

"Don't give me that, Alan," said the man in answer to the sigh. "You know I'm right, you just don't want to admit it."

"I've told you once, Bert, and I'll tell you again. The power might have gone, but that is not a reason for me to give you a free drink."

"Yes, it is. You've already told me that I can't have my sticky toffee pudding and custard because you need electricity to cook it. And, I might add, you advertise it as home-cooked and now I find out that you microwave it."

Now it was the turn of the blonde woman – the landlady,

Tony guessed – to sigh. "I do cook it myself, but then we chill it and heat it up again as it's needed in the micr-."

Bert cut her off. "That doesn't matter. What matters is that you advertise this dish as available and now it's not, so you should give me some kind of recompense. And what I want is another pint."

"And I don't care what you want. I've told you about that too. The drinks are pumped from the cellar using an electric pump, so we can't do that either! If you want a drink you can have anything we have in a bottle or can. But-," Alan continued even as Bert tried to interrupt him, "-BUT, you will have to pay for it. You can have another of our desserts. All the ice-creams are still available, at least until they melt. But the pudding is off!"

Bert mumbled something which sounded very rude under his breath and turned an appealing eye to Tony.

"Come on in, lad. You can tell him. Surely you can see that I'm right!"

Tony just looked around the room as every eye looked to him for his verdict. He thought of all that had happened to him in such a short while, and how normal this new situation seemed, and didn't have a clue what to say.

Sixteen

Despite the hobbling of the still-wounded, the group emerged from the Centre's woodland trail much faster than they'd entered it. Having shouted the retreat, Nicola had stolen the march on them and was at their head as she plunged back into the forest. Alyssa was in her arms once again but was no longer quiet. When her mother had shouted and snatched her up she had started wailing and hadn't stopped as her mother had bounced her down the path.

With no real thought for direction, just a desire to move away from the sounds of destruction which were still creeping nearer, she led the ragged band through the woods. She heard the cries of people stumbling and falling behind her, but she didn't turn and she didn't stop. Despite all that had happened this afternoon, she had managed to keep her head. Until now. This was panic in all its raging glory and she was giving it full rein. She hadn't wanted to be their 'leader', but she had taken on the role because everyone expected her to. Like so many things in her life, the expectation of others had over-ridden her own wishes and desires. But all that was forgotten now and she simply ran, to protect herself and to protect her daughter.

She stumbled and fell more than once, but each time she twisted, cat-like, to land on her back, and then with a roll she was up on her knees, Alyssa still in her arms, and then she was on her feet and running.

The noise of the beams churning the earth stopped, but Nicola carried on running. Alyssa's wailing finally calmed to breathy sobs, but Nicola kept on running. The noise of the others following her started to fade, but she kept on running.

She didn't stop until the canopy of the forest disappeared from over her and she found herself wading into a field of some kind of grain. The combination of the sudden shocking light and the impediment of the crops brought her shuddering to a stop and crashing to her knees. Alyssa struggled from her arms, seemingly wanting to get away from this crazy woman who had replaced her mother, but she didn't run off, simply stood and watched, panting, as her mother started to sob into hands which she had raised to cover her face.

Nicola did not stay there very long. Her worries of death and destruction raining once more from the skies – especially in this exposed location – were too pressing. They brought her back to herself and lifted her once more from her knees to her feet.

Alyssa was looking at her, concerned. "Are you okay, mummy?"

Nicola thought for a moment, but not for the first time, how strange it was to hear that English word, 'mummy', coming from the mouth of the child who had first called her 'mom'. Alyssa had taken to England and its version of her language much faster than Nicola could ever have expected. She had already lost almost all traces of an American accent, and Nicola knew that she would grow up sounding distinctly different to her mother. She guessed it was another reason why she sometimes felt alienated from her own child. But nothing could have been more distant now. She had almost been playing along and performing a role up until now, but all of a sudden this six year old child and her safety were the most important things in her world. She wanted time to savour this, to remember that this should have been her priority all along, but knew that any analysing would have to wait for later.

She heard noises behind her and turned. It was Stan, wading through the corn, with Dave a little way behind, and a handful of the others. She could see one or two more at the edge of the trees, but that was all. Suddenly, the guilt of her sudden flight hit her as well. The weight of all her responsibilities threatened to crush her, but she knew she couldn't let them, so she took a deep breath and buried them for the moment. There would be a reckoning later, but that was later.

"Sorry about that. Did everyone make it?" she asked Stan.

He nodded. "Yes, I think so. A few with burned legs or feet are taking a little longer, but I don't think the flying saucers, or whatever the fuck they were, came anywhere close to us in the end. It just sounded like it."

"It sure did," was her response, and she was amazed to hear a small laugh escape her mouth.

"Sounded like a mountain crashing towards us, eh?" Stan was also laughing. She could tell from his expression that he was as incredulous at his mirth as she had been. She guessed this was what adrenaline come-down felt like.

"A whole range!"

"A *continent*!"

The others were gathering around them now, watching them laugh. Some joined in and some just looked baffled or a little hurt, but Nicola couldn't stop. She laughed hard, on the verge of tears, on the verge of screaming, until she was suddenly brought back to herself, and back to sanity, by a small warm hand pressing into hers.

She looked down into Alyssa's now calm blue eyes. "It's okay, Mummy. Everything will be okay."

Nicola felt a laugh threaten at the very serious way her daughter was talking to her, but fought it back. It was enough. Her daughter was okay. The band of strangers who were looking to her for salvation were okay. She would be okay.

For the first time since emerging from the forest she looked around properly and saw, on the horizon, the top of a silo. Where there's a silo, there's a farm, she reasoned, and decided that should be their destination. If nothing else these people needed the security of walls and a roof. She couldn't guarantee that a farm would provide much more, but she could at least try and give them that.

Couldn't be any worse than the last place, she thought, and felt another giggle threaten. She straightened her face and turned to the re-assembled group. She waited till they were looking at her, then she turned and pointed to the horizon. She tried to think of stirring words to give them hope, but nothing came. So, in the end, she simply said, "Let's try there," and set off, walking slowly enough for everyone to keep up, half-leading and half-led by her daughter.

Seventeen

Sam watched Tony and waited for him to speak. He was frozen, his mouth slightly open, and she could see his eyes moving round the room, trying to find the words. Maybe, if she had been a more shallow person, she would have found this disappointing. She would have seen that he wasn't the strong man that she had thought he was. But none of this crossed her mind. She was touched by his humanity, by his sensitive nature, and so she decided to come to his aid.

"Well, I don't know the answer to your argument," she stepped forward, feeling self-conscious as all the eyes in the room turned to look at her, "but I could certainly do with a drink, even if it is from a bottle. And why don't I buy one for Bert. In fact, why don't I buy one for everyone?"

She stepped up to the bar and placed her order of a vodka and diet coke, and the others started to follow suit, the argument utterly wiped away by a beautiful young woman buying a round for the them all. She glanced over and saw that Tony had regained a little of his composure, and had moved to the back of the group, waiting his turn to place his order. She smiled at him and he gave a weak smile in return.

"She's right," he said.

"Whoever's buying is always right, lad. Don't you know that?" Bert interrupted with a laugh.

Tony gave him a flash of his teeth then continued. "She's

right. We all need a drink. I have a hell of a tale to tell you, and a little alcohol will just make it easier to hear."

He left them hanging at the end of his sentence and ordered a double Glenfiddich. Sam smiled more broadly at him, though he wasn't looking at her. She knew he just needed a moment, a guiding hand, and was glad she had been able to help him.

A few minutes later, with everyone gathered around, glasses in hand, Tony started to tell the tale. He had lifted himself up to sit on a table, to get a little height over the rest who had each drawn up a chair. Sam perched on a stool by the side of his table, looking up at him from time to time and occasionally nodding and meeting the audience's eyes to confirm the truth of what he was saying.

He told them about the helicopter crashing and the truck flying onto the road. She was impressed with his description of how he'd skidded to a halt in the nick of time and leapt from his car. He dismissed Nicola as a 'typical glory-seeking American' who had tried to save him when he didn't need it and who he had had to rescue in return.

He told them about the frying of the electrics and how he'd realised it was an EMP. And he described the arrival of the jets and the exploding crop-field, the exodus into the forest and the way in which he and Sam had been abandoned by the 'unfeeling' others. He didn't mention Bob and Janet, and some of the things he said weren't quite as she remembered them, but she was sure she'd just got it wrong. It certainly made for an exciting story and Sam realised just how much she owed this man: her life for one thing.

When he finished his story with their arrival at the pub, his audience looked at him, stunned. She looked up and he was nodding sagely at them, to tell them it was true. She turned to face them too, and copied his action.

The man called Alan, who had introduced himself to her as the landlord, was the first to break the silence with a laugh. He was on his own and it soon petered out. He looked around at the others.

"What?" His voice was high-pitched with incredulity. "You don't actually believe that codswallop do y-." He stopped, watching Bert reach into his pocket, take out a packet of small cigars, take one from the pack and light one. "What do you think you're doing?" he asked, his voice, if anything, even higher. "You know there's no smoking in here!"

Bert drew on the cigar and puffed out the smoke with a satisfied grunt. He waved it in front of him, indicating Tony. "If what the lad told us, it doesn't matter. No point worrying about lung cancer when it's the end of the world."

Alan laughed again, though this time it sounded strange. He looked round the group, appealing to them. "Come off it, Bert. You can't possibly buy this hogwash?"

Bert nodded, taking another puff of his cigar before holding it up in front of Alan. "I was outside having one of these. I saw those same helicopters flying over. Three of them. About a half hour ago. Just before the lights went out."

"What, but... but..."

"It would explain all that noise we've been hearing, too," said one of the builders. Dan, Sam seemed to remember he'd said his name was. "I know you said it was empty lorries on the main road, but I haven't really heard any traffic for ages."

"That's right," said his younger colleague. Sam definitely

remembered his name. He was Darren. His skin was extra dark in the lightless pub, but his smile was still bright. "And with the music and fridges and everything else off, we should be able to."

Everyone went still and listened, trying to hear anything from the road, but there was silence. Sam could make out some bird song, and that was all. She felt a shiver run up her back and from the looks of the others she wasn't the only one to be a bit spooked.

They all turned back to look at Tony, who she saw was waiting expectantly. He raised his eyebrows. "After all, why would I make something like that up? Do I look like some kind of fantasist? Some kind of sci-fi geek?"

"Well, you did know about that EPM thingy," Dan pointed out.

"EMP," corrected Tony, realising that he was harming his case in doing so, but unable to stop himself. "And everyone knows about that. It was in that film."

"That's right, Dan, it was."

Sam gave Darren an extra bright smile and he gave a surprised one back. She turned back to Tony and saw him looking between her and the young builder with a dark question in his eyes. She blushed a little and smiled even more widely for him.

"Well, then…" Alan broke the silence which followed this exchange. "If you're not a geek, and you're not a fantasist, then what the hell do we do now?"

"Personally, I could do with another drink," answered Bert, raising a laugh from the company.

"Yes," agreed Tony. "I think that's probably a good idea. Another drink and then we work out what to do next. We came here looking for help, shelter, and maybe a radio or a phone so we could find out what's going on. Obviously we haven't come far enough, but I'm guessing at least one of you knows the area well enough to lead us away from here, and away from whatever's happening up the road, until maybe we can find something."

"Aye," said Bert. Sam was finding his thick northern accent rather soothing, as though at any moment he would give her a boiled sweet and ruffle her hair. "Me and the missus walk all round here after our lunches. There's a path out the back which leads southeast from here. It'll take us to the Dyson farm and, if that ain't far enough, we can head down the road to the village. That should do us."

Tony nodded. "Good. That sounds like a plan. We'll have another drink and then we'll set off. We should be safe here long enough for that," he smiled around the group, pleased with himself, but none of them were listening any longer. While he'd been talking, he'd not been aware of the series of thumps that were growing steadily louder. Sam could feel the vibrations of the thumps through her stool, travelling up her spine. She turned in a full circle, trying to work out where they were coming from.

Her question was soon answered when, with a loud crashing and rending noise, a huge metal rod, ending in a flat plate came crashing through the ceiling at the far end of the pub. It had broken through the roof and the upper floor and carried on down. It smashed through the floor and into the cellar beneath, trailing slates and plaster and splintered floor boards with it. She screamed and threw herself backwards under a table, taking cover. The others were scattering, even as the monstrous metal pole ripped itself back up, out of the pub, and disappeared. No-one moved for a moment, then as a single group they all ran for the back of the pub, escaping the now-sunlit wreck of the bar for the unscathed conservatory and the car-park beyond. She emerged at the rear of the group, blinking in the bright sun, and shielded her eyes to see what they were all looking at. Striding away into the woods, in the direction from which she and Tony had originally come, was what looked like a giant metal spider. A central body the size of a small house, balanced on ten or twelve legs which sprouted from the sides at regular intervals. Each of its articulated legs ended in a flat plate.

Doreen, Bert's wife, gave out a shriek and fainted. Bert tried to catch her, but was too slow and she slumped to the ground. None of the others moved to help, they were all too busy watching the robotic shape disappearing into the distance. In fact, they were too busy even to notice the other one until it ripped down the remaining half of the pub with one of its legs and strode after its sibling.

Eighteen

Nicola led and Stan followed. He checked his watch but it had stopped along with everything else. He seemed to have been trekking across the countryside behind this woman for days.

The crops, whatever they were, seemed only half-grown, and their green stalks parted easily as they waded through them, bending and shifting then springing back into place as they passed. The ground was soft underfoot, but easy to walk on. With the expanse of green field and the blue sky and the warm breeze it should have been a beautiful day. But, like the others, Stan couldn't help hunching his shoulders against whatever might come from the skies next.

The farm appeared quickly, the silo rising into the air above them as they walked, and the building, small in comparison, huddled next to it. Stan could see an array of sheds, barns and not one, but two houses. As they got closer he could see sheep milling and bleating in a pen next to one of the barns, and a couple of dogs wandered aimlessly in the yard. A tractor stood at the gate leading into the field adjacent to the one they were walking through, its engine silent.

Everything seemed normal, except there were no people.

They reached the edge of the field and Stan went ahead to open the gate. He held it while everyone filed past then, following the 'countryside code' as he'd been taught as a child, made sure it was shut behind them. They found themselves in the main yard. Everything was silent. The gate had made quite a clang when Stan had shut it, but no-one had come to investigate.

Nicola made no move to advance further, but the whole group seemed to have started to think for themselves, as individuals. One or two of the men wandered off towards the barns, shouting their hellos.

The main group, clustered around Nicola now, rather than forcing her to be the arrowhead of their advance, wandered towards the nearest of the houses. Stan moved around the side of the group and took the role of caller-in-chief.

His shouts bounced back to him from the sides of the courtyard as they moved through it. Beyond that and the other calls and shuffles emanating from their group, there was nothing.

They reached the door of the house, and Stan found it slightly ajar. He knocked anyway, heavy blows which shook the door in its frame and opened it a little wider. "Hello! Anyone home?!"

Even as he shouted, and felt slightly embarrassed for the clichéd nature of his call, he knew that there would be no response. He knew empty houses, and this was one of them.

Still, he called again, "Hellooooo?"

Nothing.

He looked back towards the group, but no-one said anything, so he faced forward once more and pushed the door open. It was dark inside, and there was no sound at all. He could see it was a kitchen but there was no sound coming from the fridge or the freezer. They must still be within range of that pulse thing, he thought.

He glanced at the others again, still receiving nothing but expectant stares. He locked eyes with Nicola and after a moment he saw her shoulders sag and then she gave him a slow, shallow nod. He nodded back and then turned and stepped into the house.

His boots sounded loud on the bare floorboards in the kitchen. They made a hollow noise which suggested that there would be a cellar underneath. He wondered for a moment if the missing people might be hiding down there, but then realised what silly thought that was. Who would hide in an unlit cellar during a blackout?

He knew it was a daft thought and yet, as he stepped further into the gloom, he couldn't get the image out of his mind of a group of people crouching below him in the darkness, peering at the ceiling and the booming noise coming from his boots. Or maybe they weren't people, but monsters, their claws reaching up towards the sound.

It wasn't cold, but he felt himself shiver.

He took another step, now completely enveloped by the darkness of the house. He glanced back to make sure the door was still open. Sunlight was streaming in, but died where it fell.

"Hello?" he called again, his voice surprisingly flat within the confines of the room. He raised it, tried to break through the muffle which now seemed to surround him. "Hello!"

There was still no response.

His eyes were slowly adjusting to the lack of light and he looked around the room. It was a fairly ordinary kitchen. A large table filled the centre of the room. Fitted cupboards and a large cooker lined the walls. There were two doors, one of which presumably led to the rest of the house, the other to a pantry or a utility room of some kind.

Maybe it was the way down to the cellar.

Despite the invitation they presented, he didn't want to venture any further. He turned, intending to go back out and report, when he heard a noise behind him.

He spun round and could just see the door which he thought led to the rest of the house swinging slowly open. Its hinges gave a low groan, and Stan almost laughed at the horror-movie cliché of it.

The door swung all of the way open before it stopped, its base grinding into a groove in the floor. It was entirely dark beyond, and he couldn't see anyone there. Stepping closer was the last thing he wanted to do, but he made himself do it nonetheless, taking one, two, three steps towards the door.

He could make out the vague shape of someone in the doorway. As he moved further away from the doorway, his eyes were better able to make out the shape. It looked like an old lady, probably in her 70s or 80s.

"Hello?" he said, softly, taking another couple of steps. "Are you okay? The power went out, but it's okay, I'm not going to hurt you or anything. We were just looking for some shelter."

He pointed back towards the doorway where he hoped the woman could see some of the others. He glanced back to see if they were there and when he faced forward again, the woman was right in front of him.

He looked at her and felt his stomach tighten. There was something wrong with her face. Something really, really wrong. He took one stumbling step backwards, but got no further before she was on him.

Her fingers dug into his shoulder, like steel talons, and she leapt, her knees hitting him in the chest firmly enough for her slight weight to knock him onto his back, and then her mouth was at his neck and her teeth were tearing and ripping.

Stan screamed once before his throat was gone, and then he simply gurgled.

Nineteen

Tony didn't realise his head was hurt until he felt Samantha touch it. Then he winced away from the sharp pain in his scalp and turned to look at her, accusation on his face.

"Ow! What are you doing?"

"Don't be silly. It's not me. You've got a cut, you're bleeding." She held her fingers up and he saw the ruby shine of fresh blood. He reached his hand up to his head and felt the warmth of the blood and the sting of the cut. In fact, now that she had pointed it out, he could feel the trickle of the blood running down the left hand side of his head through his hair.

He traced it absent-mindedly with his fingers, unable to leave the painful gash alone, as he turned back and, like the others, watched the two metal contraptions stride away over the treetops.

Part of Tony had expected the people from the pub to all be as shocked as Bert's wife. But he guessed, like himself, they were finding this too big a thing to take in. It was almost comical watching these fantastical robots lurching through the woods, dragging trees with them when they brought their spindly legs up to take another step.

And what would be the point of running? It would only take those things a few strides and they would be right on top of them again. He guessed what he felt was resignation. He'd just been given a vision of what was happening, and it was so big that he now knew there was nothing he could do. All the planning and running was for nothing. He might as well give up, find a pub that hadn't been trampled to the ground, and find a bottle to crawl into while he waited for the world to end.

Bert was crouching next to his wife, slapping her face gently, and she was starting to come round. Doreen looked up into his face and smiled. Tony wondered for a moment what it would be like to know someone so well that a look like that would come onto their face when they woke and saw you. Then she noticed that they were outside and she remembered why and started to scream.

This acted like an alarm on the assembled group, and they all started to move at once. Alan and his wife, Charlotte, knelt down with Bert to help calm Doreen, while Dan and his young helper, and the others turned to face Tony who was standing at the rear of the group with Sam.

"Right," said Dan, a decision obviously having been taken in his mind. He looked around at the people not helping Doreen. "Get what you need from your cars. Daz, you and I'll see what we've got in the van in the way of weapons. I just know that pickaxe is in there somewhere. And we'll meet back here when we're done."

The woman with the baby, and her husband – they'd told Tony their names, but he couldn't remember them – headed to the front of the pub, where their car had luckily been spared from its collapse. The chef and waitress – again nameless in Tony's mind – headed to the car parked just feet away, at the side of the conservatory.

"And you," Dan pointed at Tony and Sam. "Well, you can help these guys get Doreen on her feet. We need to be heading away from those guys," he pointed over his shoulder to where the alien walkers had now disappeared from sight, "and this farm of Bert's sounds like the first stop. If we can get a working car there, then all the good. If not, we'll move on and see what we can find." He nodded his head at the pub. "I don't want to be here when they come back to squash the ants that ran out of the anthill."

He turned and headed after the young couple, to where his white van was parked in the shade of the trees. The young lad smiled at Sam then followed after him.

Sam moved past Tony to kneel next to the others. Doreen had stopped screaming and they were talking calmly to her, and trying to get her back on her feet. Sam got her arm under the older woman's back and helped to heave her up. She was still visibly upset, but she seemed okay.

She seemed much better than Tony felt, in fact. He just stood and watched as all these people calmly went about their business. It was like they had planned for it.

As he watched, the couple came back from the front, the baby secured in a pushchair, the woman carrying a large bag over her shoulder. Debbie, that was her name, Tony remembered. The man's name, or the baby's, still eluded him.

The chef and the waitress appeared moments later, from behind Tony. They had removed their outer-garb and were just in ordinary clothes now. Each had a bag with them and the chef was carrying a tire iron.

A noise caused Tony to turn and he saw Dan returning from the van. He and Daz had shed their high-vis jackets. Daz was carrying a sledgehammer and Dan was trundling a wheelbarrow towards them. He said something to the young couple as he drew level with them, but Tony couldn't hear it. Whatever it was, it made the man laugh and the woman smile. It was strained, but it was at least a smile.

As they got nearer, Dan called, "Here you are, Doreen, if you don't feel like walking, we can take you in this!"

The man pushing the baby nodded, so Tony assumed this was the same comment that had made him laugh before. Doreen and her attendants laughed at the idea. "You're alright, love. I just had a turn, but I'm right now." Bert patted her shoulder and kissed her cheek.

The only one not to laugh was Tony. He couldn't really believe what he was seeing. It was all so calm and orderly. How could they be so organised when his brain was whirling and his guts churning. The urge to run was trying to overtake him again, and it took all his strength to fight it.

Dan and the others finally reached them. "Only joking, Doreen, I just thought it would be easier to use this than to try and carry all these." He indicated the contents of the barrow and Tony could see an array of tools: shovels, hammers, long spanners, lengths of metal pole.

Dan took the pickaxe, and then everyone started to gather, picking up whatever they thought they could handle best. Tony managed, somehow, to unlock his legs, and approached. By the time he got there, most of the things had been taken. He reached down and picked up a long-handled screwdriver and weighed it in his hands. He didn't like the feel of it at all, but he wanted – no, he needed – to be part of the group.

"Going to take them apart screw by screw, eh, Tone?" asked Bert, and Doreen cackled. Tony felt himself blush but didn't know if he was going to burst with anger, or burst into tears.

"I don't understand what you think all this is for?" he burst out. "How are things like this going to help us against things like *that!*" He waved the screwdriver in the direction in which the walking machines had disappeared. "It's pointless, isn't it?!"

Dan simply waited for Tony's outburst to run out of steam, the others looked from one to the other like spectators at a tennis match.

"You're right. We can't do anything about them. But we're heading in the opposite direction and maybe – " he spun the pickaxe in his hands, " – maybe we'll find something else that we can do something about. And I wouldn't want to be without something in my hands should that happen. That okay with you?"

Tony dropped his gaze and nodded. Sam, now holding a large claw hammer in one hand, stroked his shoulder and arm with the other.

"Right, then," said Dave. "Let's go."

Twenty

Despite her better instincts, Nicola's first reaction to Stan's scream was to take a step towards the door. She let go of Alyssa's hand and took another step, then stopped. She looked back, but Dave, his face white, had already reached out to take the girl's hand. He nodded to her.

It occurred to her that it should be him going in after her friend, not her. But it was too late to protest, her legs were already taking her inside.

Even as she crossed the threshold she tried to work out why she had been so willing to take on so much responsibility. Everything that was asked of her, she balked inside, and then stiffened her back and did it anyway. What was she trying to prove? And who was she trying to prove it to?

She didn't have time to think much more. She stepped into the dark of the house and her eyes adjusted enough for her to see Stan lying on his back on the floor with what looked like a wild animal gnawing at his throat. There was a lot of blood on the floor. There was no way he was still alive.

She wanted to run to him, and she also wanted to run away. Instead she simply stood still, hoping that the creature wouldn't notice her. But, of course, her entrance had made a shadow on the floor. Whether the creature only now noticed it, or whether it had noticed but had been too busy to care, Nicola didn't know. Either way, it stopped its attack on Stan and looked up with a snarl.

Nicola realised with a shock that what she had taken for some kind of wild beast, a large dog perhaps, was actually a person: an old woman. Her left eye was gone, a red spongy mess in its place, and her mouth was slathered with gore. The woman growled at Nicola, followed by a pre-human scream which erupted from the old woman as she leapt.

Nicola uttered a scream in reply, but not one of fear, one of rage. All the tension she had been bottling up came out in a warrior's cry as she swept her arm across and knocked the woman against the wall in mid-flight.

From somewhere outside, Nicola heard her daughter calling for her, but that wasn't important right now. The wizened creature who was climbing to her feet was her priority. Nicola backed into the kitchen. She knew she was moving away from the door, and away from the light, but she needed to let her eyes adjust, and she wanted to find something she could use against this nightmarish hag.

The woman was back on her feet. Nicola could see that her right arm was hanging at a strange angle, but it wasn't stopping her as she approached across the darkened room.

Nicola retreated, her eyes fixed on the woman, until her back collided with a worktop. She reached behind her, trying to find a weapon of some sort. Her hand closed on the handle of something heavy and, as the woman leapt again, Nicola brought round whatever it was she had grabbed and smacked the woman across the head with it. It was a cast iron frying pan and once more the woman was sent sprawling.

She was back on her feet more quickly this time, almost as though the beating Nicola was doling out was giving her more strength. Nicola strode over to the woman as she rose and struck her again with the pan, driving her to the floor. She hit her again and again, keeping the demented creature on the floor, even as her arms flailed up, trying to scratch or grab.

Slowly, even as Nicola's arm started to tire, the woman's arms dropped, and she lay still. Nicola stood over her, panting, the pan still held at shoulder height ready to hit again, but the woman finally lay still.

Nicola realised that she was making a small keening noise with each laboured exhalation. She let the pan drop to her side, but didn't let go of it, and backed away from the body of the woman, watching her as she moved towards the door. She stopped briefly at Stan's body, but his throat was laid open and he was obviously dead.

With a sigh which threatened to become a sob, she turned and walked out through the back door. As the sun hit her she became aware of the blood and tissue spattered on her arms. Some of it was from the woman and some of it, she thought with a shudder, was from the bits of Stan's throat the woman had still had inside her mouth.

She fought the urge to retch and raised her hand to shield her eyes from the sun.

What greeted her was not what she expected. There was no Dave, no Alyssa, no group of followers waiting to hear the news of what had happened. The courtyard was once again deserted.

Twenty-one

The sun was getting lower in the sky. It was high summer, so it was still hot, and the sun would be up for a while longer, but already Tony could feel the day slipping away. He tried to remember what time it had been when the truck had come flying towards him. About three, he reckoned. From the position of the sun, he thought it was maybe now about six. Could all of this have really only taken three hours? It felt like a lifetime.

He knew he wasn't the world's greatest thinker; or feeler for that matter. More than one woman had accused him of being emotionally stunted. He knew they were right, but hell, he'd been happy. Or he thought he had been. In the last few hours he had felt more emotions than he could remember feeling in a long time. Most of them had been fear, but still, he felt alive in a way he couldn't remember since... since... Well, a long time.

In another respect it felt like nothing more than a few minutes. Everything had happened so fast. He was driving and then he started running and it seemed like he would never stop.

It felt strange to just be walking now. Doreen had recovered well and was full of bluff and bluster, with no sign of needing to walk slower. The path they were on cut between two fields. One was full of some kind of crop, the other was grass with cows grazing, oblivious to anything else happening in the world. They would take a mouthful of grass and then lift their heads and gaze mournfully at the party walking past.

Tony walked in silence. At the head of the group Doreen and Bert were keeping up a constant stream of chatter with Dan and his apprentice. Tony had stayed at the back, not wanting to take part. Sam hung back with him, and despite his reticence, Tony was glad.

He didn't know if she was aware of his need for isolation, or if she was lost in her own thoughts, but she didn't say anything and he was glad of that too.

He kept running over the events of the afternoon, wondering what was going on. Was this really an alien invasion? He couldn't come up with any other answer. He ran over all the things he had done and realised that he felt ashamed. He'd acted like a coward and that didn't fit with his image of himself at all. He'd just wanted to run and hide and save himself. He remembered, as though it was months ago, the exchange in the woods, and he wondered where Nicola was and how she and her group were faring. He wondered if they'd seen the same walking machines as he had and what she had done about it. He was sure she would have done more than stand and stare in awe and horror. She would have been like Dave, he was sure. She would have made plans and done her best to keep the people around her safe. She wouldn't have hung back and let everyone else take care of her.

For some reason, Tony's thoughts drifted, for the first time in a long time, to his mother. Could it really have been so long? It seemed so very recent. She had always taught him to be brave and strong. That was her mantra for him during her illness. She never showed weakness and she didn't want to see it from him either. He knew that if she had seen him today she would have been disappointed in him.

His father has been weak. Maybe that was where Tony had got it from. Maybe he could blame his genes for his need to run and hide. When his mum had become ill, his father had retreated from both of them, leaving Tony as her partner in her sickness. His father had always liked a drink, but when she started to go downhill he had started drinking more and more. Tony thought of his earlier urge to give up and climb inside a bottle of whisky and felt a hot blush creep up over his face. He was just like his father and he found he hated himself for it.

He really did wonder if Sam could read minds as he felt her slip her hand into his. He didn't say anything, didn't even turn his head, but he gripped her fingers and held on as if her hand was the rope that was keeping him from falling to his death.

"What I don't understand," Tony realised that Dan had slowed down, allowing the group to pass him so he could come and talk, "is why here? What is there here in the middle of nowhere that those things – whatever they are – would find so important? I mean, I could understand them attacking London, or New York or Washington, or whatever, but why here?"

"Maybe they are attacking all those places. How would we know?" Sam responded before Tony could even process the question.

Dan nodded. "True."

"And, after all, that's what they do in all the movies, so it has to be the case, doesn't it?"

Dan gave a soft laugh and nodded again. Tony couldn't

decide if he was jealous of the look Dan was giving Sam, or of the fact that her brain still seemed to be working well enough to not only think about their situation, but to joke about it too.

"I wonder-." Tony was only aware he was going to speak when it happened. "I was driving down the road and, well, I have to admit I wasn't paying a lot of attention, but I'm sure I saw a sign for an army base."

Dan nodded. "Yeah, there's a few of them round here. An army base, and an airforce one too. And, of course, Salisbury Plain isn't a million miles away from here. Why? What are you thinking?"

Tony wasn't sure what he was thinking. Something was rising from the depths of his brain and he was still trying to make out the shape. "Well, it just occurred to me. If you were going to attack somewhere, why would you start with a city? Okay, if you wanted to just arrive here and kill everyone that would be great. You've got a dense population of people and all that. Blow up London and you take out millions of people in one go." He could start to see where his thought was going and he didn't like it, but he kept going.

"But what if you wanted to keep the people alive? Okay, you might lose one or two along the way; collateral damage. But if you wanted to remove resistance and have the people left behind, then you'd start by attaching the military targets."

Dan was nodding and the look of respect he gave Tony gave him an almost physical jolt which he could feel run through his spine. "That makes sense. You take the enemy by surprise, take out their weapons and their fighters, and then you just have the ordinary population to deal with.

You remove the initial resistance and also the people who might be able to come up with a plan to fight back."

"Exactly."

"Well, that's good," Sam interjected.

"Good?" asked Tony. "What's good about them coming in and wiping out anyone who could stop them?"

"Well, it means they're worried. They feel that the army, or the airforce, or whatever, actually have the ability to harm them. They're not coming in as an overwhelming force unconcerned about what we might do to them in return. They're trying to take out any resistance before it can start because they know it could stop them."

"Okay, that makes sense. That's a good thing." Dan smiled at her, but Tony no longer cared. His train of thought had taken a different route.

"Yeah, that's good. I mean, then we just need to hole up, find somewhere safe, and wait until our guys win. But, if they don't, there's something that worries me."

"What?"

"Why do they want all the people? If they're not here just to kill us all and take over the planet, then what do they need us for? Slaves? Subjects?" He glanced back over at the cows staring over at them. "Or food?"

Twenty-two

After that they walked in silence. There didn't seem to be anything they could say to Tony's question. They now seemed to have some idea what was going on, maybe even an answer to why those walkers hadn't stopped to kill them, but without understanding the bigger purpose there was nothing they could do. In the end Tony's earlier comment had been right. All they could do was try and find somewhere safe and hope that the good guys won.

After Tony's final question, Dan had moved back to the front of the group, a sombre expression on his face. She didn't know if he would tell the others the conclusions they'd come to, but Sam doubted it.

She slipped her hand back into Tony's, unsure just when that had become uncoupled, and they continued to walk in silence.

The path twisted between the fields, cutting south and then east as it followed the fields.

The farm appeared on the horizon sooner than Tony had expected. He started to seriously doubt that it was far enough away to have escaped the electro-pulse thing. It was a cluster of buildings around a courtyard. Sheep were cropping grass in a field next to one of the barns and a tractor stood silent in the centre of the yard.

As they grew closer, Tony saw two dogs lying in the shade by the open door to what seemed to be the farmhouse.

They passed through the gate at the end of the path, Dan holding it for the party and shutting it with a clang behind Tony and Sam. They all stopped at the edge of the yard and waited, but no-one came out to greet them. The whole place seemed deserted.

Dan walked back through to position himself at the front. "Hello?" he called.

There was no response.

The group walked slowly into the courtyard, listening carefully but hearing nothing but silence. Dan and Daz set off towards the house, the dogs rising to greet them, friendly rather than threatening. The chef, the waitress – Tony thought he really should learn their names – plus Debbie and her family, waited in the middle of the yard, watching them. Tony decided not to just wait to be told what to do, but to take some kind of action which wasn't just running away.

With his screwdriver gripped in his hand he approached the nearest barn. The large door was ajar, but he could see nothing in the inner darkness. He glanced back and saw Sam was following him, a few steps behind. He nodded to her and then stepped in through the open door.

There was a smell of rotting grass inside which made Tony wrinkle his nose and try to breathe through his mouth. Some shafts of light were shooting through gaps in the roof and walls, and Tony realised the barn was quite old and a little dilapidated. As his eyes grew accustomed to the darkness, he made out large shapes in the room. He raised his screwdriver protectively, and nearly yelped when he felt Sam press against his back, but then realised that the huge metal shapes in front of him were another tractor and a combine harvester. Around the sides were smaller metal machines which Tony imaged could be attached to the tractor for cutting grass and ploughing fields.

He stepped in further, walking round the side of the harvester.

He jumped when Sam called out, "Hello, anyone here? We're friendly, don't worry!"

There was no response.

The rounded the back of the harvester and were faced with the rear wall of the barn. Tony could just make out various tools – spades, hoes, axes – hanging from hooks on the wall. He thought about replacing his screwdriver with some a little more wieldy, but decided to wait until they found the farmers and ask them, rather than simply stealing.

He turned back to Sam, who had followed him round. "Looks like there's no-one h –"

He stopped, mid-sentence, as a grating noise came from below the harvester.

He stepped back, turned and grabbed an axe from the wall, then faced the source of the noise.

"Hello?" he called, his voice shaking despite his best efforts to control it.

He crouched down and squinted under the large metal machine. There was a two foot gap under this end and he could see a hatch of some sort, which must lead down to a cellar.

He held the axe in both hands and waited, as the hatch opened a little further.

A pale hand emerged and thrust a stick out to keep the hatch open, and then the face of a young man was looking out at him, fear etched on his face.

"Have they gone?" he asked.

Twenty-three

"Has who gone?" Tony asked, crouching down to address the young man face to face. Even as he did so, they heard a shout from outside. Tony jerked and fell back onto his bottom and the man yelped. His face disappeared from the open trap-door and it slammed after him. Sam could hear a bolt being thrown.

"What?" asked Tony. He looked from the hatch to where the shout had come from and back again. Sam could tell he was torn between the two and felt something akin to pride that he so obviously wanted to do something. She liked Tony, but she had been slightly ashamed of him on a number of occasions already. She had thought at first that he was strong, but then she started to wonder if she'd been mistaken. Something seemed to have changed in him, though. He had a sense of agency that had been missing, and she was pleased to see it.

She stepped back from where she had been half-crouching behind him.

"I'll go," she said. "You try and get him to come out again. Something's happened here and I think we need to know what it was."

Tony had climbed back to his feet and was wiping the dust from his trousers, and rubbing his bottom where he had fallen onto it. It was a comical vision, watching him massage his own behind, but Sam didn't smile. Tony nodded and she quickly stepped around him, around the side of the harvester and headed for the door.

The brightness of the light stung her eyes, forcing her to blink and squint. She looked around and saw that the others, Andy, Sandra, Charlotte, Debbie and Ryan were still standing in the middle of the courtyard. Ryan was still holding onto the handles of little Heidi's pushchair. Of Dan and Darren there was no sign, but all the others were looking towards the open door of the farmhouse.

She rushed over to them. "What's happened?"

Andy, the chef from the pub, glanced at her only quickly before fixing his eyes back on the doorway. "Dan and Daz went in to see if anyone was in there. Maybe someone was hurt, I think Dan said. There was nothing, and then one of them just shouted."

"It wasn't a shout, it was a scream!" Charlotte was upset, and Sam noticed that Sandra seemed to be holding her back. "Alan went in to see what was going on. I told him not to."

"A scream? Was it one of them or someone else? Did they say something or was it just a scream?"

"It sounded like Dan," volunteered Sandra. "He cried out, that was all. Then Alan ran in."

"Should we go and help?"

"I don't think so," Andy shook his head. "If there's something in there that the three of them can't handle, then I don't think there's much point the rest of us rushing to our death."

Sam looked at him, incredulous. "And would you want them saying that about you if it was you in there? God, are all men cowards?"

She ran for the house, and Charlotte broke free from

Sandra and followed her. As they reached the doorway, however, they saw Alan running towards them. He was looking behind him and nearly ran straight into them. They moved back, half catching him as he stumbled on the threshold. He was quickly followed by Dan and Daz bundling through the door after him.

Alan threw his hand out and dragged Charlotte by the arm towards where the others were standing. Daz did the same for Sam, leaving Dan behind them, watching the door warily.

"Is it following?" Daz called back to him.

"I can't see it! I don't think so!"

"Move back, you saw how it could leap, for God's sake!" called Alan.

"I can't see it!" Dan sounded panicked.

"You won't." The voice came from behind them. It was quiet and unsure, but it carried across the courtyard, causing even Dan to turn.

Tony had emerged from the barn with the young man – not much more than a boy, really – who had been hiding under the harvester. It was the boy who had spoken.

"I don't think they like the light. I'm not sure, but I think as long as we're out here in the sun, we're safe."

"Who? What? What is in there? What are you talking about?" Sam had caught the panic that was emanating from the three men who had been in the house.

"It's my mum."

Twenty-four

Nicola knelt on the tarmac of the road running past the farmhouse with no memory of how she had got there. The pains in her knees told her she had dropped to them, but the last thing she could remember was being in the courtyard with no sign of anyone. No sign of Dave and certainly no sign of Alyssa.

She remembered screaming but then nothing until finding herself here, panting, in the middle of the road. She got up, needing to search, needing to find her daughter, but her legs were weak and wobbly. She sucked in air, steadying herself, and started to remember running from building to building around the farm, searching, and realised that she had already tried to find her daughter and been unsuccessful. From the position of the sun she had lost an hour or more.

She stood in the middle of the road, looking up and down its length, trying to decide what to do next.

She walked slowly back into the courtyard, more of her memories of searching returning to her. There had been no sign of disruption, no sign of a struggle, no explanation for the disappearance of thirty or more people.

She looked again but could see nothing that she wouldn't expect in a farmyard: scuff-marks on the cobbles; scatters of grass and miscellaneous animal feed; muddy patches with paw and hoof marks printed in them; various types and amounts of animal dung; nothing unusual.

She walked back around the buildings, remembering more clearly now her dash as she went in and out of them all. She hadn't stopped to consider the possibility of meeting another creature like the one in the farm house, but she had been lucky and the rabid pensioner seemed to have been a one of a kind.

She walked back into the darkness of that kitchen once more, driven by a morbid desire to look again at the woman. Part of Nicola wanted to make sure that the woman had been real, and that she hadn't been hallucinating. Another part wanted to make sure that the woman hadn't moved.

The body was still there. Her head had been caved in by the weight of the pan Nicola had wielded, and she could see bone and brains showing. She looked closer at the damage which had been there before Nicola had encountered her. Even in the thick of the battle she had noticed that the woman's left eye seemed to have been gouged out, but amongst the mess of Stan's blood which had been trailing from her mouth, Nicola had failed to notice the large part of the woman's own neck which seemed to have been bitten away.

Not for the first time today, she wondered just what the hell was going on.

She made to leave the kitchen, remembering again the scene that had greeted her when she first came in: the old lady gorging herself on Stan's throat, and she realised something that had been tickling at the back of her mind. Stan? Where was Stan?

She went over to the patch of floor where he had been. It was increasingly dark in the room. The sun was dropping down below the trees. But she could still see the patch of blood that had been left on the floor when the woman had torn his jugular. She could see that so clearly because there was no Stan in the way. He was gone.

Then, looking closer, she saw the hand-prints he had made in the blood when he had struggled back to his feet. And she could see the footprints which led from the puddle to the door in the far corner of the kitchen. A bloody handprint was smeared on the white woodwork of the frame.

She started to follow after him. He had only been hurt and needed her help! And then she stopped. She looked down at the copious amounts of blood washed over the floorboards. No, he had been more than hurt. He had been dead.

She didn't know what the hell she was going to do next, but she knew that following the dead into the depths of a strange and increasingly dark house was not one of them.

She went back out into the light, listening carefully for any movement. She had seen how fast the old woman could move, but at least she was small and light. If whatever had happened to her had happened to Stan, she did not want to be present if he decided to take to the same kind of activities.

She stood in the farmyard for a moment, and then came to a decision. Her daughter was not here. Neither were any of the other people she had been travelling with. If they weren't here they were somewhere else. In that case, she decided, she also needed to be somewhere else. It was the only way she would find them.

She walked from the farmyard back to the road where she had come back to herself after her panicked fugue. She looked left and right up the road and with nothing to choose between them, turned to the right and started walking.

Twenty-five

"Dad had only just started the tractor when the power went out. At first he thought it was just the tractor playing up. It's getting old and we can't afford a new one, and it does cut out from time to time. He had the bonnet open and was jiggling the wires when I came out to tell him that the power had gone off in the house."

They were sitting on a grassy bank on the edge of the field beyond the farmhouse. It was raised enough that it would be last place around to lose the sun, and James had told them he thought they would be okay in the sun. Dan had also approved because it was high enough to see anything coming to them from any direction. They had sat themselves in a circle around the boy to hear his story, but Dave told them to keep an eye out for anything. He didn't say what and he, Daz and Alan still hadn't told the others what had happened in the house. All Tony knew was that these previously fearless men were badly shaken and didn't want anything creeping up on them. Although James was facing him, and Dan was on the far side of the circle, as they listened Tony kept looking behind him, just in case.

"When I told him he came in and checked the fuses and tried all kinds of things, but nothing did any good. Then I told him that my phone and my iPod had both gone off at the same time and he looked worried. I didn't know what was going on, but he said he was going outside to have a look around."

James shook his head and looked to be on the verge of tears. But he looked so tired; Tony wondered if he had already cried himself empty. "I wonder if he'd have been all right – if we'd all have been all right if he'd just stayed indoors with me and mum." He shrugged and gave a humourless laugh. "Or maybe I'd have been trying to rip your throat out too."

At this, Tony felt Sam gave a start next to him. *Rip your throat out?* What was the boy talking about? Tony wanted to confront him, make him start talking sense, but Sam must have realised he was approaching an outburst. Her squeeze of his hand stilled him and he carried on listening.

"He was gone about ten minutes and when he came back in, my first thought was that the tractor had blown-up. He was red, like he had been badly burned. His skin was blistered and even seemed to be smoking. He didn't smell of diesel, though, but like cooking meat. He smelled like the middle of a really good barbecuing session." Now he did give out a low sob, but he carried on talking. "It actually made me hungry, but then the thought of food made me sick. I just stood there, looking at him, feeling all these crazy things. I couldn't move. But my mum could. She didn't notice, and neither did I, the crazy look in his eyes, nor the fact that his throat had been ripped wide open and his shirt was covered in b-b-blood."

Debbie, who had left her baby with her husband to sit next to the boy, put her arm round his shoulder and held him to her while he sobbed. It was soft and muted: tired, and it soon ran itself out.

He wiped his eyes with his thumbs. "Sorry," he mumbled to her.

"Don't be daft," she said, and pulled a tissue from the pocket of her jeans, which she passed to him. He wiped his eyes again, and blew his nose. He went to offer it back, but then realised that she probably didn't want it now. He held it in his hands and looked down at it as he continued, talking to the tissue.

"My mum ran over to him, asking him if he was okay, asking what had happened. He didn't say anything, but when she got to him he kinda snarled and then he b-bit… He bit her. Here." He touched his throat and then pulled his hand away as though burned. "And he kept biting. And biting."

His breathing hitched, and Debbie gave him another one-armed hug, but he pulled back and nodded to show he was okay. "He dropped her on the floor and there was blood all over the place, and then he turned to me. I was frozen in place. I should have run, or hid, or something, but I couldn't think; couldn't believe what I'd just seen. He took a couple of steps towards me and then I realised that I could barely see him. His skin was really smoking and by now it was almost black. With his next step he…. well, he crumpled, melted. A second later there was nothing left but some kind of dirty slime."

He looked up, his expression asking everyone to believe his tale, even though it was plainly insane. Tony wanted to disbelieve, to call him a liar, but he couldn't. He'd seen enough strange things today that he thought he would believe anything now.

"What happened then?" asked Sam, softly.

"I still couldn't move. I just looked at the mess on the floor which used to be my dad, and the body which had been my mum. I couldn't even scream or cry or anything. I just stood there."

He drew in a deep rattling breath. "And then she moved."

Twenty-six

The shadows of trees and hedges lay full length across the road as Nicola walked. There were the sounds of birds and the occasional rustle in a hedgerow which she thought could have been a squirrel or a hedgehog or a field mouse. Part of her brain kept trying to throw the word racoon into the mix, but she beat it back. Hell, for all she knew the noise was made by rats. They had rats in the country, didn't they? She wasn't sure.

She realised she wasn't sure about anything. She'd been back in the country for a couple of years, but her brain still thought in American. All her references, all her knowledge of laws, and customs, and even wildlife were for a country thousands of miles away. She was adrift in a country which, when she lived in the US, she had always claimed as her own. Now she realised she didn't know it at all. Hell, what does a 14 year old know anyway? They know their friends, their back-gardens, the boys at school and that's about it. Before she'd left she'd never really had to interact with the world, she'd always had her mum for that.

She would have said her mum and dad, but her dad had always been busy at the college, even at weekends, so it had just been her and her mum. She'd seen much more of him when they got to Boston. His position at Harvard had more prestige and, strangely enough, that came with a lighter workload. But by then it had been American society he had been introducing her to.

She missed the familiarity of New England, but was still sure she had made the right decision to come back to the old one. She couldn't have stayed. The whole place was too tied up with her and Rob. She'd met him at 18 and he'd taken over from her father as her interface with the world. Everything she had seen and done as an adult had been done with Rob, and when she had found out about him and Crystal, she had known immediately that not only did she have to leave him and finally have a life of her own, uncontrolled by him, but she had to leave her adopted home. She needed a fresh start in a new place with new people, where she could recreate herself on her own terms.

What kind of a name was *Crystal* anyway?

She realised that she was going over all this old ground in her head to stop her from thinking about what was happening around her; to stop her thinking about Alyssa, and Stan, and everything, but she didn't care. She didn't want to think about it all, if she did it would stop her moving forward. And if she didn't move forward, she would never find any way to resolve any of this.

That was the way she had rationalised her move back to England. She needed to get away, and after all those years of Rob showing her off as his woman from the 'mother country', she knew where she ought to belong. Once her mind had been set, she had just put her head down and made it happen. She'd found her job, found her house, and a school for Alyssa, and she had moved them with nothing much more than the force of her stubbornness.

And now she was left wondering if it was the right idea. She was a fish out of water. Every turn she took she found that although this country seemed to speak the same language, it was a twisted, through-the-looking-glass version where everything meant something else. She kept getting things wrong and the moment she opened her mouth her voice gave her away as an intruder; an interloper. She had thought she would be coming home, but instead she felt like she was living abroad. She was an ex-pat in her own country.

She realised she was no longer simply walking, but was striding down the road. Despite the long summer evening, the high hedges and trees which bounded the road were making it darker and darker and she was all but rushing into it.

She started to slow, but she was still going too fast to stop when a figure came crashing out of one of the hedges, leaves and twigs flying in front of it to rain against her face.

She just had time to make out that it was a man before she collided with him in mid-recoil and the two of them fell onto the road, entwined. Nicola kicked and screamed, trying to separate herself from her attacker, pushing back on his face to keep his teeth from her neck.

In turn the man was pushing at Nicola, trying to keep her away from him. His hand forced under her chin and pushed her head back.

"Get off me, you fucking thing!" he shouted, and she realised she knew the voice. It was Dave.

She stopped fighting. "Dave?"

He stopped, mid push, and peered at her in the gloom. "Nicola?"

She nodded, easily pulling back from him now they had both stopped struggling. "Thank God," she panted, still recovering from the surge of adrenaline which his appearance had caused," I've been searching for you. What happened? Where did you-."

She stopped because Dave had ignored her question. Now freed from the tangle he had leapt to his feet, grabbed her arm, and pulled her up with him.

"No time," he panted. "Later. Later. Now... Run!" And he set off down the road, dragging her nearly off her feet.

She stumbled for a few paces until she got her feet under her, and then she was able to run with him. He let go of his hand and they raced down the road. They were running so quickly it was difficult to speak, but Nicola managed to pant, "What? What?"

Dave didn't respond, just kept his head down and carried on running. But Nicola got her response when she heard the sound of the hedges tearing behind her and at her side. Other people were breaking through, but all of them, men, women – some of whom Nicola recognised from the group she had led through the woods – even children, had loose flesh hanging from their throats and a range of other injuries. One or two of the figures looked strangely misshapen, almost not human at all, but she didn't stop to examine them. She just ran and ran, Dave at her side, desperately trying to outrun their pursuers.

Twenty-seven

"When she did, I ran," James continued.

Sam watched the contortions his face was going through as he struggled on with his story. She wanted to go and put her arms around him, but Debbie had taken that role and she didn't want to crowd him. Everyone else was silent as he spoke.

She couldn't speak for the rest of them, but part of her was having trouble believing his story. The rest of her, the part that had seen planes bomb a farmer's field, which had seen two people flattened by half a jet fighter, that had seen giant metal spiders destroy a pub that she was sitting in, knew he was telling the truth.

"I didn't know what she was going to be like when she got up, but I didn't think it would be good. I'd seen what dad had done to her. I'd seen the blood run out like water from a tap. I'd seen the mess he'd made of her throat, and I'd seen her drop to the floor like a bag of spuds. She wasn't breathing after that, I was sure of it, but that didn't seem to stop her."

He paused for breath, panting, reliving the experience. Debbie rooted in her giant bag and came out with a bottle of water which she passed to him. He drank and calmed a little, then continued.

"She was fast. Between the first flicker of movement and me being out the door can't have been more than a few seconds, but she was on her feet and after me all the same.

"I ran from the house, presuming she was after me. I ran all the way across the yard, vaulted the gate, and kept going. But then I realised that the gate had made a loud clang when I had cleared it. The bolt gave way last year and now we just use a hank of rope to keep it shut. It means it's loose, but it does the job. If she was after me, surely I would have heard it. I risked looking back and she wasn't there. No-one was. I was alone.

Finally, someone spoke. Sam was vaguely surprised that it was Tony. "Where was she?"

"Still in the house. I went back, you see. It took me a while and I went really slowly, but I needed to know. When I got back there I could hear her in there, moving around in the dark. I called out, and she didn't say anything, but when I stepped closer to the doorway, she leapt out, but only as far as the shade would allow. When she hit the sunlight she jumped back. That's why I thought we would be safe out here. Whatever they are – whatever she's become – they don't like sunlight, I don't think."

His story told, he stopped talking and his head dropped down between his shoulders like a robot with flat batteries.

The others looked around, eyes meeting, expressions grim. One or two glanced up to the sinking sun, and Sam knew what they were thinking, because she was thinking the same. If sunlight was protecting them, then they needed to get somewhere safe before it went dark.

"Okay, I get all that." It was Tony again. "What I don't understand is why, if they like the dark so much, you were hiding in the cellar under the barn. Surely that's the darkest place around."

James nodded, his head rising slowly with each nod, as

though he was re-inflating himself with a pump. "I heard someone coming. After I'd worked out that I was safe in the sun, I didn't really know what to do. I was just wandering around the farm, trying to think of a plan, when I heard noises coming from the road. It sounded like engines, but not cars. I don't really know what they were, but I didn't want to wait and find out. The cellar is pretty well hidden. If you don't know it's there, it's hard to find. There aren't any other entrances, no windows to break in or doors to force, and it had a large bolt on the inside. Dad said it was used by smugglers or something, but I think he was making that up. He always says that –." He faltered as he remembered again that his father was dead.

"Anyway, it seemed the best place to hide, so I hid."

Twenty-eight

Their pursuers were fast, but Nicola and Dave were faster. Her legs soon felt like lead and her lungs were burning, but there was no way she was slowing down. After a hundred yards or so, new zombies had stopped bursting from the hedge, so they no longer had to run the gauntlet of their emergence, merely out-distance them.

They ran side by side, Nicola occasionally taking the lead, but Dave managing to keep up despite carrying more weight than she was.

Slowly, foot by foot, they started to outrun the creatures following them. She scanned left and right, checking for any new ones emerging from the deeper shadows at the sides of the now darkened road, but none came.

The road twisted and snaked, and signs of pursuit disappeared, but neither of them slowed down. Nicola wanted to ask so many questions. She wanted to know what had happened to Dave and the group. She wanted to know how so many of them had become – well, whatever they had become – so quickly. Most importantly, she wanted to know what had happened to Alyssa.

Even as they had started their panicked race, she had scanned all the scarred and mangled faces she could see; terrified that one of them would be a twisted, staring parody of her daughter's. None of them had been, but until she knew from Dave what had happened to them, she didn't want to hope that this was a good sign.

They rounded another bend, still racing, and a patch of late summer sun lay across the road. It was the gateway of another farm. The trees and hedges stopped, and the large open farmyard allowed the last rays of the setting sun to reach them. The cracked tarmac glowed red as though a furnace door had been opened, but Dave didn't pause. He reached out and dragged Nicola through the shining portal of the gate, facing straight into the red searchlight sun.

He slowed. "Sun... Sun..." he panted, his breath catching in his throat. "Sun hurts them. We're... safe... here."

"Yes, but... only for... a moment. Just...a ... rest."

"Yes. Yes. A moment." Dave stood in the full glow of the sun, his skin bloodily lit, and tried to gain control of his breathing. Nicola found the pain in her lungs was already starting to clear, and she raised her head to look around her.

A group of dark silhouettes was advancing on them out of the sun. With all that had happened today, she could be forgiven for flashing back to Close Encounters of the Third Kind, but when she wiped her hand across her eyes, they refused to disappear. She reached for Dave's arm, getting ready to repeat his favour and dragging him into another run. Obviously Dave's fact about the sun was wrong. But before she could move, one of them spoke.

"Nicky? Is that you? My God, what happened?"

She peered into the light, trying to make out features. "Tony?" she asked, recognising the voice.

The man-shaped shadow at the front of the group moved round so he was now half-lit, and she saw that it was indeed the man she had left in the forest only a few hours ago. A few hours which felt like a lifetime. In the red light, he seemed to have a patch of black covering the side of his face. She guessed, after a moment, that it might be blood.

"Yes. It's me." He stepped forward and she could see him more clearly. He looked like a different person; older and calmer. Then she realised what was different. It wasn't the head wound or the dirt on his clothes. He wasn't staring at his cellphone. She almost laughed at the banality of the thought. "What happened?" he asked again.

"Do you know?" she asked, unable to find the words to describe the images in her head. "Have you seen?"

"Zombies? Yeah. Well, we've heard." He pointed to one of the others who still stood in the scarlet glare. She didn't see which one. "There's one in the farmhouse, apparently. Why? Did you see one?"

She snorted. The edge of condescension she remembered from the afternoon was still there in his voice, but she didn't care anymore. "Seen one? I beat one to a pulp with a frying pan, and there are another – what, thirty?" she asked Dave, who nodded. "Thirty, following us. They were chasing us down the lane. We just stopped here for a moment's rest."

A male voice sounded from the group, "Thirty? Shit?"

A larger figure stepped forward to where Nicola could see him without squinting. "How far behind you were they?"

"Not far," said Dave. "They won't follow us in here while it's still light. But, listen, when it gets dark they-"

The other man cut him off. "We know. They don't like the light but they love the dark."

"What are we going to do?" asked Nicola.

"We were just discussing this and we think we have a solution. It's not the best, but we hope it will do." The man turned and led them towards a barn. The rest of the group followed and they entered into the almost complete blackness of the building. A young voice said, "Hold on." There was a rattling noise followed by the scratch and fizz of a match being lit. A teenager was standing by a bench at the side of the barn, holding a large lantern. He applied the flame to the wick and the room grew measurably brighter. "This way," said the boy, and led the way round the side of the tractor and the red side wall of a Combine Harvester.

Reaching the rear, he gestured under the body of the monstrous contraption. "There," was all he said.

Nicola watched as the large man who had spoken to her last in the yard crawled under and opened a trap door in the floor. He took the lantern from the boy and held it down into the hole. For a moment, they were plunged back into darkness, and Nicola felt her skin crawl. She was sure, for that moment, that there was something in the dark with them. Then the man pulled the lantern back out and the feeling went away, but she thought she heard noise in the distance. Could it be the sound of feet on the road? Maybe in the farmyard?

"It's okay," said the man. "There's room for all of us if we squeeze in. There's no food or water, but we'll be okay overnight."

He stopped talking and cocked his head. Tony started to ask something, but the man held his hand up to shush him. Nicola realised that the footsteps weren't just in her imagination. He could now hear them too.

She stepped back and peered around the side of the harvester. There was still the glow of sunlight in the yard, but it was even darker now. If they were somehow allergic to sunlight, they wouldn't have to worry about it for much longer. She didn't wait to be asked, but rushed through the darkness to the door. Dave was at her side. Working in silent accord, they pulled the barn door shut, and slotted a large beam she had seen when the boy had lit the lamp into two hooks on the backs of the doors. She rooted around on the bench from which he had taken the lantern, and found some lengths of rope. She passed them, working by touch, to Dave, and the two of them lashed the beam to the hooks. It wasn't totally secure, but hopefully it would do.

She had just finished when she felt a groping hand reach hers in the darkness. She drew breath to scream, but Dave shushed her. "It's okay. It's me," he whispered then pulling on her hand led her back round the side of the barn. The group of people had climbed down into the cellar, and soft light spilled out of the hole into the darkness of the barn.

Dave helped her down into the trapdoor, hands reaching to help her down, and then he followed after her. He pulled the hatch shut and the boy was at his side, helping him bar it.

The cellar was about twenty feet to a side, so was large enough for them all, if not exactly palatial.

She moved down and found a wall to sink down next to, finally aware of her legs shaking from the run, and her body aching generally. She wondered where Alyssa was as the night settled in, and hoped with all her body and spirit that the girl was okay. She was still full of questions, but like the others, she knew that this was not a time to speak.

She looked around at the group she had joined and was surprised to see a woman carrying a baby. She hadn't noticed her before. Nor had she seen the older couple, or seen that the young blonde who had attached herself to Tony earlier was still with him.

They all sat round the edges of the underground room,

their backs to the earthen walls, the lantern in the centre of the room, lighting all of their faces. They looked like she felt – shaken and drained. But there was a stoic quality which helped her keep calm, for now. But she knew it was going to be a long night.

No-one spoke, no-one moved, except for the mother rocking her baby. Every ear was cocked, listening for sound from above. They had done what they could. The headlong race of the afternoon had led them here, and now they finally had to stop and see what happened next.

In the solitary light from the old paraffin lamp, they waited.

Twenty-nine

Sam woke with pain in her back and neck from sleeping on the earthen floor. The room was in darkness, as it had been before she fell asleep, the paraffin having run out after only an hour's light.

They had sat around the room, whispering occasionally to remind themselves they were not alone in the solid darkness. Mostly, though, they had listened. They knew when night had fallen because they heard banging and groaning coming from outside. It wasn't any attempt to get in. If those creatures knew there was anyone inside the barn, they didn't have the wit or co-ordination to get in. After a while the banging stopped and the screaming started.

It was loud and terrified and when it started Sam felt everyone in the room become still and tense. It took her a moment to work out, but then she realised it was the sheep who had been in the field next to the barn. The – god, she hated even to think the word – the *zombies* were slaughtering them. She wondered if they would become zombie sheep, but she didn't dare air the thought. She didn't know whether she'd laugh or scream.

All too quickly the noise stopped. After that there was nothing but silence.

They had waited, all of them trying to be as alert as they could, but the silence simply stretched into the night. Without a way of telling the time, the seconds and minutes stretched ever longer. Eventually they felt they could talk.

At Nicola's insistence, Tony told her about what had happened since they last saw her. Sam noticed that his story seemed more accurate than when he told it in the pub. If anyone else noticed, they didn't say anything.

When he finished, Nicola started to tell her tale. She spoke calmly, her voice almost inflectionless, even as she spoke about her daughter's disappearance. She had told of Dave and the others disappearing from the yard, and the way in which he had returned, chased by the transformed group of which she had been the leader. Sam wondered how she felt about having lost so many people who had looked to her for guidance, but again she said nothing.

She finished her story with the moment of reunion with Tony and Sam, and fell silent. Sam was surprised she hadn't asked Dave to tell his story. Surely she must want to know what had happened to her daughter. She was about to say this, and then realised that Dave might not have good news. In fact, he might not already have told her because he didn't want to tell her that her daughter was dead.

The room filled up with unasked questions and unspoken thoughts, until finally Dave started talking.

"It happened almost as soon as Nicola ran inside. We heard a scream from her, and then there was a shadow over the sun. It was one of those huge metal spider things that you were talking about, Tony. I guess it must have been while you were in the pub telling your tale, or you'd have seen it. Hell, maybe it was even the same one that crashed in on you. I don't know, I didn't stay to watch. It was moving straight towards us. I scooped Alyssa up into my arms – that was when she called to you, Nick – and then I was running. It only took me a moment to realise that the others were following me." He paused, and Sam wondered if he was also thinking about the way these people had cast him as their leader and he had led them to, well, to their living deaths.

"I led them down the road to the left. It twisted to the right and took us in a straight line away from that huge thing. But it was moving so fast, it was over us before we knew it. And then... it was over us and gone. Just like you said, Tony. It didn't look at us twice, just carried on over the countryside. Soon it was gone, but we were still running. We slowed down, and I would have come straight back for you Nick, I really would, but we'd reached another farm. I thought it made sense to see if we'd come far enough for power to be working before we came back for you. It would only be a minute."

He fell silent, and a pregnant stillness swelled to fill the room. Then he sighed and it blew like a chill wind through the silence, causing Sam's hair to raise on her arms and her neck to prickle.

"We didn't know about the darkness, you see. I looked in the farmhouse, taking a spade I found in the yard with me just in case. But it was deserted. After that, we were just complacent. We started looking the barns. A whole group went into one and..." Again he let out a huge sigh. "And they didn't come out. We didn't hear any screams or anything, but I think there must have been a whole family in there, maybe some farmhands too. I think they jumped the group as soon as they walked in and ripped out their throats before even one of them could scream."

Sam heard him shift and realised he had turned to Nicola. There was a tone of pleading in his voice. "I would have gone in after them. Maybe I could have done something, but Alyssa wouldn't let me go and kept asking for you, so I stayed outside. The rest of the group – all of them – grabbed whatever they could find and went in after the first lot. Oh, God!" He let out a wail which was immediately muffled as someone – Nicola maybe – put a hand over his mouth.

Eventually he calmed and his breathing slowed enough to continue. "This time there was screaming. It sounded like a massacre. God, they weren't soldiers, or fighters or anything. They were just people. They went in, without fear, to try and help strangers, and..." He trailed off.

"I waited. Alyssa was crying for you, but I waited. I hoped that one of them - at least one of them, for God's sake – would come out. But they didn't. Well, not as they had been.

"It all went quiet and then a man came to the doorway. His head was split and not only was his throat gone, but so was most of the side of his face. I could see his – his – his teeth and his tongue through the side of his face. He watched me for a moment and then he leapt. I grabbed Alyssa and started to run. He followed me across the yard. God, he was fast. But soon I heard him slow. I looked back and stopped. He had slumped to his knees. I saw his skin catch fire and he melted to jelly right in front of me."

He paused, but no-one filled the gap. Sam thought she heard a sob from the far corner but couldn't tell who it came from.

"That was when I ran properly. I headed across the yard, past the house, over the fields. At the top of one of the fields I found a shed of some sort. It had no windows, just stone walls, a roof and a single thick door. I took Alyssa in there with me. She was screaming blue murder by then, and

I hid."

"You have to understand, I couldn't believe what I had seen, and I couldn't... I just needed some time. I needed to work it out."

His voice was shaking so hard that Sam couldn't understand how he could keep going, but somehow he did. "I should have come back. It didn't take me long to work out that it was sunlight which had done for that... that... thing. But I couldn't. Once we were in there with the door locked, I just wanted to stay. I just wanted to hide until it all went away."

Sam heard him turn to Nicola again. "Alyssa quieted down. There was some hay in there and she went to sleep on it. I sat and tried to think what to do. It was only when I realised the light was fading that I knew I needed to come back and find you, if I could, before it got dark."

He started crying quietly as he continued. "I left her sleeping. I didn't think we'd end up here. I thought I'd find you and we'd go back and we could all be there when it finally got dark."

Sam imagined this new pause was to allow Nicola to say something, but there was only more of that silence. When he realised she wasn't going to say anything, he carried on. "It wasn't that dark when I left. It would have been okay, but I hadn't thought about the long summer shadows. In order to get back to you I had to pass through the farmyard, and the shadows of the buildings were long enough that they had come out of the barn and were milling about. I saw them before they saw me, and I ran through them, but they followed. The shadows were long enough, from buildings and then from trees and hedges, that they only ever had to be in the sun for a moment at a time. I think some of them didn't make it, but you saw how many were still with me when I reached you. I'm so sorry I left her. I'm so sorry. I – I –"

He had stopped talking and just cried.

Nicola hadn't said anything more for the rest of the night.

Thirty

With no way of telling the time, in a cellar under a barn, they had no way of knowing when it was light outside. They tried their best to judge it, but James had, with everyone's consent, opened the trap door three times before he told them he could see light coming through gaps in the barn's walls.

They emerged, stretching and groaning, into the half-light of the barn. Nicola could tell that it was another sunny day outside as the light streamed in, causing dust to dance. Feeling the weight of her legs under as she walked, she stumbled to the big double doors which she and Dave had roped shut the night before. In the gloom it was hard to tell, but she thought that the door looked untouched. Everything was as it had been. She guessed they had been right in the night. The zombies weren't trying to break in. The banging they had heard was just the less co-ordinated among them hitting the barn on their way past.

The others came up behind her and the large man who had introduced himself as Dan helped her to remove the ropes and the beam.

They pushed the doors open, causing them all to blink in the brightness of the day.

From the height of the sun, Nicola could tell that it was already mid-morning. Maybe ten o'clock. They hadn't been able to see the light before then because the barn was still in the shadow from the buildings beside it. They'd spent longer than they'd needed to, waiting for the sun to rise high enough to be seen from inside. Nicola cursed under her breath. They had probably been safe to leave for hours. And each of those was 60 minutes more that she could have been using to look for Alyssa.

She stepped straight out into the sunlight, squinting as she looked around. The others emerged behind her. Despite her desire – her need – to go after Alyssa, she couldn't help being drawn, like the others, to the field which bordered the barn. It was a massacre. There were parts of sheep strewn all over the field. Not one had been left alive. Bite marks covered the torn flesh.

She turned away, not wanting to look. Her fear that the same fate might have befallen Alyssa was too strong, and she felt that she would be tempting fate if she stared to long. If she confirmed that this was real, then maybe that would be too.

She stepped back from the rail, behind the others. "Right," she said, in a firm voice, to get their attention. She didn't want them looking at the slaughter anymore either. They turned and looked at her, and she realised that once again she was the leader. At least now it was justified. She was the one with something to lose. They were all in danger, but she was a woman with a mission.

"You don't need me to tell you what I'm going to do. I'm going to find my daughter and you –," she pointed at Dave, "you're coming with me. The only question is, what are the rest of you doing?"

Tony spoke first. "I'm coming with you."

The blonde girl, Sam, looked at him and Nicola could see surprise on her face. She studied him for a moment and then turned back to Nicola. "Me too."

"And me," said Dan. His friend Darren nodded his agreement. Where his mate went, he would go.

The others just looked at each other for a moment, but said nothing. Finally, Bert spoke, "Me and the wife'd just slow you down. I think you want to move fast and that'd be no good." His wife nodded.

Debbie didn't need to say anything. Even as they had been talking she had calmly raised her top and started breast-feeding young Heidi as if this was a perfectly normal activity for such an occasion. However, her eyes met Nicola's and she gave her a hard smile and fierce shake of the head, one mother to another. If she wasn't going to come, neither would Ryan, so that was that.

Alan and Andy looked at each other, their arms around their respective partners and nodded. Alan spoke for them, "I think we'll stay with this lot. They could do with looking after, I reckon, and you've got the three Ds: Dave, Dan and Darren."

"Okay, then," said Nicola when she was sure she had everyone's answer. The only one who hadn't spoken was James. He was looking back over his shoulder into the mess of sheep-parts that used to be field. "Well, we know where we're going. The only question left is where are you lot going to go. James?" He flicked his head back, almost as though caught doing something he should feel guilty about. "I take it you're going with the rest of them?"

He paused, and she knew what he was thinking. "You can't stay. I know it's your home, but what if they all come back tonight? These people need to find somewhere safer and more comfortable than the cellar of a barn, and they've only got the day's light in which to find it. You're going to have to show them. This is your neighbourhood after all."

He looked at her, stricken, and she felt her heart go out to him, but she couldn't let him shirk this burden. "You need to find them some food, some shelter, something that can be sealed against attack. Can you do that? Is there a town or somewhere near here?"

He nodded, and she saw his Adam's apple moving in his throat. "Where is it?" she asked, as kindly as she could without giving in to the welling tears in his eyes.

He pointed out of the gate to the right, the opposite of the way she and her group had to go. She nodded, that seemed right.

"Okay, you're going to take them there. Don't worry, you can do this. You'll be fine." He nodded. She wasn't sure he believed her. Hell, it was a crappy pep talk. As long as he did what he was told, that was enough for her. He didn't have to like it.

"We should get some food, first, if we can." Tony said. Nicola nodded. It was going to be her next point.

"Yes, we're going to have to go into the house and see what we can get. Matches, candles, anything like that would be useful. Food, yes, and anything else that might be useful."

She saw Sam turn to James and place her hand on his arm. She spoke to him softly and he answered. She asked something else and he nodded, slowly, unwillingly.

"What is it?" asked Nicola. She knew her voice was overly harsh, but she really didn't want to have to wait any longer than she had to.

Sam looked over at her, and Nicola could see a rebuke in her eyes. "I was asking him what size feet his mum had. They were 5 the same as me. So I thought I'd see if I could get some better shoes for running over fields." Her words were defiant, challenging Nicola to make something of it.

Nicola nodded. It was a good idea. "Yes, any clothing or even sleeping bags would be useful. Whatever there is."

She looked around and everyone was nodding. She glanced over her shoulder at the house. "But before we do that, we need to make sure it's safe in there."

Thirty-one

They approached the house warily. Dave and Dan had taken the lead, and for all that Tony was feeling brave, that was fine with him. They'd all armed themselves, either with the tools they'd had the day before, or with new things found in the barn. Tony had replaced his screwdriver with the axe he'd picked from the wall just before he found James. Dave and Dan each had a pickaxe, Darren his sledgehammer. Alan was carrying a length of metal bar, and Andy had, of all things, a golf club.

At a time like this, traditional gender roles had been asserted, and the women stayed outside in the safety of the sun. All, that is, except for Nicola. She was carrying what looked to Tony like a rusty sword, but which James had informed them was a broken blade from the old threshing machine. Whatever it was, she carried it with purpose, and Tony for one would be keeping out of her way. He guessed she was keen to get moving, but with them having to go through the house first, he was happy to take as long as necessary.

Dave and Dan waved for the others to hang back and they went in on their own. The others waited outside, listening intently for whatever sounds they could hear. The guys' boots made a heavy noise on the floorboards which grew more muffled the further they went in. There was silence for a moment, and then one of them called, "It's okay in here, you can come in."

They entered. Nicola went ahead and the others followed, with Tony bringing up the rear. It was surprisingly dark, the small windows letting in little light. He looked around. There was nothing much to see. It was a kitchen. There was a wet patch on the ground where he presumed James's father had fallen, but nothing else to suggest disturbance. As far as he could tell the zombie horde hadn't even been in here last night. Maybe it would be okay, and they wouldn't find anything. They could just get in and get out.

Darren and Dan started to open cupboards. They found large reusable carrier-bags and started filling them with food. Nicola and Dave headed for the door which, presumably led to the rest of the house. Andy and Alan followed, and so did Tony.

The hallway was also untouched, and Tony felt himself start to relax. Andy and Alan went through the open door into the lounge and Alan reported it empty. "There are some rucksacks, though. We'll take them back to Dan and Daz, they can fill them with food. Easier to carry that way."

At the bottom of the stairs, Tony found himself directly behind Nicola and Dave. He wasn't keen on being so near the front, but didn't really have an option. The three of them climbed the stairs. It was dark at the top. As they neared the landing, Tony realised this was because all the doors to the rooms had been closed. They reached the top without anything jumping out at them.

They didn't confer and they didn't split up. Nicola took the lead and headed back along the short landing to the front room. She paused with her hand on the doorknob and looked back at the others. Dave nodded and, after a moment, so did Tony. She turned back and flung the door wide, stepping back to give them all room to swing if they needed to.

Nothing moved. The room was empty of zombies. Not, thought Tony, that many could have fit in there. It was a small box room which had been used for storage. It had all kinds of things piled inside. Nicola let out a deep breath, and Tony realised he had also been holding his. He let his out slowly, through clenched teeth, in a quiet hiss. She nodded to herself, then spoke quietly, "Okay, this is good. There's bound to be stuff in here we can use. Let's check the other rooms first and then see what's in here."

Dave nodded and Tony just prepared himself to perform this nerve-wracking action over again. He looked around at the doors and counted. Another four times.

They turned to the door immediately on their right, the room over the lounge. Again, there was a pause before Nicola threw the door wide. Again, there was nothing. The room beyond was obviously the main bedroom. It had a large, unmade bed, and male and female clothing dotted around.

They stepped inside, but a quick inspection told them this room was empty too.

The next two rooms – James's bedroom and a home office – were also empty, which just left the last door.

This was typical, thought Tony. He'd seen horror movies. He knew how this worked. The tension is on the first door, by the last one the heroes are getting relaxed and – BAM – that's when the monster gets them.

They all seemed to be thinking the same thing, because, here in real life, rather than being relaxed, they were even more on edge.

Once again Nicola checked with them, and once again they confirmed they were ready with a simple nod. She reached for the handle, drew a deep breath, and flung it so far open it banged off the wall and started to close again.

Unless the porcelain was possessed, there was nothing in the bathroom, either. The house was clear.

They all sagged with relief; Tony going so far as to clutch the banister.

Dave gave out a low chuckle, which became a laugh. Tony joined in and then, reluctantly but inevitably, so did Nicola. The tears streamed down their faces as they let go of their tension.

It took them a while to get hold of themselves, and by the end the laughter was no longer fun. There was a hard edge to it all and Nicola seemed on the verge of tears. Tony went to put a comforting hand on her arm, but Dave was ahead of him. He put his arm round her shoulder and she leant her head on him as her laughter became a sob, which became a sigh.

She stood like that for a moment, then straightened.

"Okay, then," she said. "Let's see what's in that front room."

They moved back down the landing, and Nicola went in and started hauling things out. They found small packs containing sleeping bags, more rucksacks, wet-weather gear, a box of candles and some wind-proof lanterns, and all kinds of camping equipment. As Nicola passed the things out, Dave started to pack them into a rucksack. Tony watched.

When the first rucksack was full, Dave passed it to Tony. "Take this down and come back for the next one."

Tony didn't argue at being ordered around in this way, he

just complied. He hoisted the rucksack onto his back and headed downstairs. There was a hairy moment when he leant too far forward and the weight of his pack nearly sent him tumbling, but he grabbed the banister and kept going.

He walked through the kitchen where the other guys were still packing food into the rucksacks they'd found in the lounge. He left the pack he'd brought and headed back inside.

He had just reached the landing again when he heard a shout from downstairs. There was a loud crashing, more shouts, and then a huge shape was bounding up the stairs towards him. It was a large man, travelling on all fours like a giant dog. His head was lolling from side to side and Tony could see it was because half of his neck was missing.

Tony screamed.

Thirty-two

Nicola turned as she heard the noise from downstairs. She realised immediately what it was and started to struggle from the pile of debris that she had built around her legs. Her 'sword' was leaning against the door frame and she grabbed it, just as Tony screamed. She watched as a huge shape leapt at him. He took a step backwards and fell, full length, onto his back, knocking the wind out of his lungs and cutting off his scream.

The large zombie landed on the other side of Tony, turned, snarled and charged at her and Dave. Dave had dropped the rucksack he'd been holding and reached for his pickaxe. He misjudged, however, and knocked it to the floor. As he bent to retrieve it, the zombie leapt again, straight towards Nicola.

She swung with her blade, bracing her feet for the impact. It sank into the side of the creature, stopping it mid-leap and knocking it against the wall. It kicked out at Dave as it fell and he was knocked sprawling onto the floor of the main bedroom. As the creature hit the floor, the blade, stuck deep in its side, was pulled from her grip. As she lunged after it, she realised that she recognised the face of the creature which, even as she looked at it, was scrambling to its feet to re-launch its attack.

"Stan?" she asked, incredulous, unable to control her instinctive reaction to reach out to this man she recognised

The thing that had once been Stan grabbed her arm and pulled her towards him. She let out a yell and tried to pull away, be he was too strong. It cocked its head, baring its teeth, seeming to take a slow meticulous pleasure in what it was about to do. It was almost as if it remembered her enough to make this a very special occasion.

She frantically tried to pull back, but to no avail, as Zombie Stan reeled her in, his mouth aiming for her throat. Just as he was about to sink his teeth into the tasty morsel that he had found, his head flew sideways and collided with the wall, and his arms let her drop.

"There," said Tony, with an air of finality. He had regained his feet and clapped the creature on the side of the head with the flat of his axe, crushing part of its head. He stared down at it with an air of triumph, and looked completely surprised when it started to get back to its feet, snarling even louder.

It took a step towards Nicola, who had retreated back into the box room, and then Dave's pick-axe swung through the open doorway from the main bedroom and the pointed pick part disappeared through the zombie's face, carried on through and came out of the back of its head.

Dave planted his weight and pulled, yanking the zombie which had replaced his closest friend and pulled it through into the bedroom. Sunlight was streaming through the windows and when it hit the creature, it started to emit a gurgling scream. Its skin started to bubble and slide from its bones.

With a cry, Dave pulled the axe from its head, moved behind it, and with a foot planted in the middle of its back, sent it crashing through the windows, tumbling to the yard outside.

Nicola and Tony, who had made their way into the room in time to see this, could hear screaming from outside, but it soon stopped. Nicola imagined this was when the huge shape which had fallen from the house became nothing more than a steaming puddle of goo.

She could hear shouts and footsteps from below, the others coming to see if they were okay. For the moment, she couldn't care about them. Dave, having ejected the monster, had stopped in the middle of the room, staring at the empty space where the window had been. Nicola was vaguely aware of Tony slipping from the room to assure the others they were okay. She stepped forward and turned Dave towards her. He looked stricken.

"It's okay, honey. It's okay," she crooned, reaching up to stroke his face.

He let the pickaxe fall from his hand and it hit the floor with a thump. "It was... It was...." he murmured.

"I know, honey. I know. But it wasn't him. He was already gone. That was just some *thing*."

He finally looked up, into her eyes. She could see him pleading with her.

"It wasn't him." She was more definite now. "He was gone. That was just the thing that wanted to kill us all, and you saved us."

She was nodding at him, over and over, trying to convince him. "You saved *me*," she said softly, and then she was kissing him.

It started as a soft, comforting kiss, but quickly became more. The tension and the stress travelled through both of them, culminating in a fierce mashing of lips and scraping of teeth. It was animalistic and intense and neither of them was aware of Tony coming back into the room. He stopped and watched them for a moment, then left without saying anything or making a sound.

Thirty-three

They came out of the bedroom only seconds after Tony left them. He had waded into the box room and was carrying on packing and sorting, finding things they needed. They didn't say anything about what had happened, and he didn't tell them he'd seen them, he just carried on with the task. They took the objects he passed them and continued filling rucksacks.

When Alan and Andy had come rushing upstairs to check on him, Nicola and Dave, Tony had told them that they were all okay. He said what had happened, and they told him that it had come up through a trap-door in the cupboard under the stairs. No-one had checked there. Daz had slammed the door and was waiting for the others to come back down so they could go down and check, but they reckoned that if there had been more, they would probably already know.

The thing had emerged from the cellar, crashed through the door of the cupboard and knocked Andy off his feet as he walked from the lounge to the kitchen. He'd then headed straight upstairs, as if he had a particular reason to be there.

Satisfied everything was okay, the others had gone back down to help Daz, and that was when Tony had walked in and seen Dave and Nicola.

He didn't know what to do. More importantly he could

feel himself reacting inside but didn't know what to make of what he was feeling. All he knew was that he hadn't liked watching them. He wasn't embarrassed, it just wasn't something he wanted to see.

He backed out silently and went back to the box room to sort things out, thoughts spinning round his mind like bluebirds around a dazed cartoon character's head.

With the three of them working on the things in the room, it didn't take them long to fill the 5 rucksacks they found. Tony did find a sixth at the bottom of a pile, but when he put in a camping lantern it fell through where the bottom should have been and the glass smashed on the floor. He swore much more loudly and vehemently than the damage required. They had, after all, already packed four of the things successfully.

They had mostly been packing in silence, Tony still mulling over his thoughts, but Nicola had spoken once to comment on the fact that they were lucky to have found a family of hoarders. Tony grunted a response and the silence fell again.

Dave was doing the duties of ferrying the full packs downstairs again, leaving Nicola and Tony alone from time to time, but Tony had nothing to say to her and she seemed lost in her own thoughts. She didn't seem to be as set on finding her daughter, and he did wonder idly, as he tried to understand his own inner conflict, what she was thinking about. He guessed she was worried what she would find when they got to the shed where Dave had left her, and part of her didn't want to have to face the awful possibility.

How could she kiss him after he abandoned her daughter? Tony suddenly wondered. Just as quickly he dismissed the thought and went back to his rummaging. He had shifted and sifted most of the things in the room, but he just wanted to check for any last thing that they might need.

That was when he found the shotgun.

He had been moving things off the narrow bed which had been pushed under the window. Things had been piled high on it, and he'd had to clear the floor in front to get to it. Lying under a pile of old coats, the last thing before the mattress, was the gun. Next to it was a box of cartridges.

He couldn't think why it was stashed away up here. It looked very suspicious. He would have thought, if it was for farming purposes — culling badgers or whatever — that it would be somewhere within reach. It felt… hidden.

Whatever the reason, he was glad he had found it. He lifted it up, surprised at how heavy it felt and how cold the metal was on such a warm day. He turned with it in his hands and heard Nicola give a gasp. She knew, as he did, that they had just found the single most useful thing that they could. She held out her hands to take it from him, but he pretended not to notice and held onto it. He turned back and grabbed the box of shells, and then started to make his way back out of the room. As he passed Nicola he pointed with the butt of the gun to the last of the rucksacks which was on the floor, leaning against her legs, he asked, "Can you manage that on your own?" But he didn't wait for the answer and headed off downstairs.

Thirty-four

Nicola followed Tony downstairs, unsure quite what was going on. Something had obviously happened to him when the zombie had attacked, but she wasn't sure what. Maybe it was the scream and the falling over backwards. He could be ashamed of himself. But he had stood up and smacked that zombie with his axe – the blunt side, okay, but he had still saved her life. Maybe he had discovered something about himself in that moment of heroism and it was a new-found determination she could feel. Whatever it was, she knew she should ask him, but she couldn't find the words and her mind was whirling too much to search for them.

Why had she kissed him? That was what she kept asking herself. If there was anyone in the group that she should hate, it should be Dave. He had taken her girl – when there was a threat, admittedly, but one which never became anything more – and he had locked her up and abandoned her. She ought to want nothing more than for him to lead her to the shed and then never clap eyes on him again.

But, somehow, she couldn't criticise him for what he had done. She could understand exactly why he had done what he did, and knew that she would have done the same in that situation. And when she had seen the look on his face after he had had to kick the undead version of his best friend through the window, she had just wanted to make it better for him. He looked so torn, so anguished, so full of emotion, so human. So unlike Rob.

She had just wanted to soothe and comfort him, but then she had been kissing him. It wasn't a decision she had taken, it was just something that happened. It had been nice. There had been a lot of other feelings mixed up in that kiss, but it had been nice. It was the first kiss she had had since Rob and she realised how much she missed the feeling of another's lips on hers.

But even as she was kissing him, her hands pulling his head hard against hers, she had known that she didn't really want to be doing this. And now it had happened, she didn't think she wanted to do it again. She didn't know why, but instead of feeling something new open up inside her, it had just left her feeling awkward.

They had broken their kiss and she had been unable to look at him, simply turning and returning to where Tony had already re-started the job that she should have been doing.

And now she was standing in the doorway to the box room, with Tony already downstairs, and she still wasn't moving. She couldn't understand it. She had woken up knowing what she needed to do and how she was going to achieve it. But as she had started rummaging through the belongings of other people who were only recently, dead, she had felt her purpose leaking away. Her mind just kept filling again, as she had known it would, with the sight of the field full of dismembered sheep. In her mind's eye, each limb, each pool of blood, each splintered bone was Alyssa's. Her daughter's face appeared in her mind with a thousand different expressions of pain, horror and anguish; and every eye in every face accused her.

She hauled the rucksack from the floor and onto her

back and made her way downstairs. She knew she had to carry on with the task ahead of her, but her dread weighed her down. In the kitchen they were dividing the things that had been found upstairs more evenly, and interspersing food with more practical objects. Nicola suspected that they had packed more things than they would need, but didn't want to take any chances.

She stood in the doorway and watched them, the weight of the rucksack threatening to bring her to her knees, but she was unwilling to let it drop. Following the checking of the house, and the zombie attack, the others who had waited in the courtyard were now clustered around the back door. Nicola watched as they chatted and swapped objects back and forth, sorting what they would each need and who was capable of carrying what. Tony had also set himself apart from it all. He had taken a chair and placed it against the far wall. He was examining the gun. So far he had worked out how to open it, and was now examining cartridges which he had taken from the box. As she watched, he started to slide them into the gun: one, then two. He closed the gun with a click, and she saw a look of satisfaction pass over his face.

He looked up and saw her and his face went blank.

She stepped into the room and finally swung the pack from her back and let it thump to the ground. She took a deep breath, then, "Okay, then. How are we getting on?"

Andy looked up from where he was sliding bottles of water into one of the packs. "Not bad, we should have enough stuff to keep everyone comfortable and fed for a few days if needs be." He glanced around then back to Nicola, "We should be good to go in a few minutes. We just need to sort that one out." He pointed to the pack Nicola had brought down, and Dave stepped over to take it from her. He glanced up into her face, but she couldn't read his expression. She looked away.

"Okay, good." She turned and called out through the doorway, "Sam, if you want to come in, I'll show you where the bedroom is. We can get you some shoes."

Thirty-five

Sam was conscious that everyone was now waiting for her. She and Nicola went upstairs quickly and she was able to find trainers which fit her when she added two pairs of trainer-socks on each foot, and also to exchange her 'little black number' for a pair of drawstring ¾ length 'shorts' and a t-shirt which wasn't too baggy.

Nicola had left her to change, but all in all it had taken less than 5 minutes. She walked back into the kitchen, looking more practical but a lot less glamorous, she felt. She had even tied her hair up with a band she had found on the dressing table. She didn't know if it was the new look, or just something what had been simmering, but as soon as she walked in, Tony stood from his chair at the side of the room, walked over to her with the shotgun held at his side, slid his left hand round the back of her neck to cup her head, and kissed her.

It was a soft and sensuous kiss, which grew a little harder and more passionate as it continued. Sam was aware that all movement in the room had ceased and imagined all eyes watching them, but she didn't care. She didn't know if it was the pressure of the situation, or just hormones which didn't know when to shut up, but she had wanted Tony to kiss her almost as soon as she had first placed her hand on his shoulder back in the woods. She melted into the kiss, and felt her body mould to his, but he didn't change. He stood, straight as a plank, holding her head to his, and kissed her until she finally had to break away, to breathe. She looked into his eyes, still surprised at the suddenness and publicness of what he had done. She didn't know what she expected to see in his eyes – some softness, some affection, perhaps – but they were flat and fathomless, like a poisoned reservoir. She almost pulled away, but his fingers massaged the back of her neck a little, and she saw his face soften into a smile.

"Sorry," he said, the smile seeming to fit itself over his features, rather than being part of them. "I just needed to do that."

She tried to think of a response, but before she could he had turned back to the others, who looked away and tried to pretend they hadn't been watching.

"We ready?" he asked them.

A last couple of things were swapped between bags and then they all agreed that, yes, they were ready.

Nicola seemed, after dawdling far more than Sam would have expected, to have found her urgency again. She grabbed a bag and swung it onto her back, and marched out of the kitchen, causing the group outside to have to back out of her way. The rest of them followed.

Once back into the open, everyone split into their two groups without having to be told. Dave, Dan and Nicola were carrying the packs for their group. Andy, Alan and Ryan had the other three. A couple of small bags had been hung from the back of Heidi's pushchair, too.

There seemed little to say, now they had finally reached this point. Dan and Daz wished the others from the pub good luck, and the sentiment was repeated across the groups. And then they picked up their weapons and walked.

At the gate there was another round of farewells, and then James was leading his group off to the right, towards the village, and Dave was leading the others to the left, back the way he and Nicola had come the night before; back to Alyssa.

Thirty-six

Nicola was angry. She knew she had no reason to be, and that her mind should have been focussed on her daughter, but it was anger which drove her now. She just wanted to find her daughter and get her away from all this to somewhere safe; somewhere where they could wait out whatever it was that was happening. Somewhere away from Tony.

She had no reason to have been shocked and angered by the way he kissed Sam, but she was, and she hated herself for it. When he stood up and did what he did, she knew immediately what had happened. He had seen her and Dave, and it had made him... what? Jealous? Something like that. And he had then kissed the girl in retaliation. That was what she was angry about. She wasn't jealous for herself. She was just sad for the girl, who had obviously taken a shine to him, for some unknown reason. He had used her to try and get back at Nicola and the girl was going to be heartbroken when he cast her aside. She knew his type; she knew that would be his pattern.

Okay, so stressful times brought people together who would normally never look at each other, and maybe some of that was what was going on between Tony and Sam. But it was no excuse for treating her like that.

As they walked away from the farm, Dave set the pace, but Nicola soon moved up to join him. Dan and Daz followed behind, with Tony and Sam bringing up the rear. Nicola glanced back and felt a fresh jolt of anger as she saw they were holding hands. Sam was smiling, but Tony's face was set.

A minute later and she could no longer worry about such things. They reached a place where a whole length of hedge had been torn down.

Dave stopped. The others caught up with him as he spoke, "This is the place where I came out last night, or as near as dammit. We could go back by the road and round, but I think this is quicker and I'm fairly sure I remember the way. It's not particularly hard, but it is cross-country. That okay with everyone?"

They all agreed and again, he led the way. They stepped through the hedge and stopped. Like the sheep by the barn, the cows in this field had been ripped apart. Splashes of gore and bovine body parts littered the fields. Nicola ignored them, stepped around Dave, and carried on going. She didn't look back to see if the others were following.

They did, and Dave was soon walking at her side again, guiding her to a gate which led to a field with similarly butchered sheep in it.

They crossed two more slaughterfields before they reached one containing crops. At the edge of this one, the ground started to rise and, as they climbed, Nicola could see a roof appear on the horizon.

She turned her head towards Dave, not breaking stride. "Is that it?"

"Yes," he replied and then watched as she doubled her pace, taking the hill as if it wasn't there.

The others started to drop behind, but all other thoughts had left Nicola's head. She no longer cared what Tony did with his life. She didn't care if Sam got hurt — she was a grown up and had to make her own mistakes. She didn't care what Dave might assume about her and their shared kiss. She didn't even care that he had abandoned her daughter here overnight. All she cared about was getting into that shed and rescuing what would be a very frightened, very hungry and very bewildered little girl.

Despite the weight of the pack on her back she sprinted up and over the brow of the hill. She rounded the side of the shed and stopped.

The door was not just ajar, it was completely gone. In the efforts to remove it, whatever had wanted to get in had torn the boards of the door into so much kindling. The pieces lay scattered across the grass in front of the shed, and she could see spatters of blood on them.

She was still standing there when the others arrived. They were out of breath, but that was not why no-one said anything. They all just stood ranged around her and looked at the same scene of devastation which had halted her.

Finally Dave stepped forward. He looked into her face as he passed her, making sure it was okay for him to do what he was doing, but she didn't say anything to stop him. She wasn't sure she could say anything at all.

He stepped into the shed and then straight out again. She waited for him to tell her about the mess of limbs and intestines and blood which was all that was left of her daughter. He took a breath to speak and she all but cringed before the blow that she was sure was coming.

He shook his head. "Nothing. She's gone."

Somehow, she found her voice. "No... body?"

He shook his head again, and walked over to her. He took her hands in his and she was reminded of their moment in the bedroom. He looked into her eyes." Nothing. No blood, no body, nothing. Maybe, wherever she is, she's okay."

His voice was soothing, but she knew exactly what it was he wasn't saying.

She nodded at him, acknowledging, but not agreeing. "That's true. Or maybe she was screaming and they heard her. They broke down the door and – hell, maybe she ran for it – but more likely they dragged her out, they tore out her throat, and next time it goes dark my own daughter will come looking to eat her mother's brains."

She never raised her voice, but she saw him flinch at her words anyway. She felt bad for a moment. He was taking all this as his fault, but he hadn't caused any of it to happen. He had just been trying to do his best. He might have messed up, but he hadn't intended it. It occurred to her to say this, to try and relieve his guilt, to put aside her own feelings to make him feel better. But she didn't. She didn't have the chance.

She was just working out how to phrase what she wanted to say when the sky went dark. She looked around, expecting to see one of the giant metal spiders which she had been told about, but had yet to see. The transition from sunlight to shade was so sudden that she thought it must have been cast by something. Instead, as she looked up, she saw thick dark clouds- as thick as smoke, but too high up and moving too fast – covering the sky.

"Look!" Daz, who had ended up at the back of the group when they clustered at the front of the shed was pointing beyond it, back the way they had come.

The empty shed and its raft of possible meanings was forgotten in the moment. Nicola moved round the shed to look where he was pointing.

She looked out, over the fields and woods which they could see from their vantage, and could see the line of the A34 cutting through the landscape. In breaks in the trees she could see the snake of stalled cars, and had to force herself to remember that it hadn't even been twenty-four hours since she had been there.

Beyond that she could see the blasted and blackened landscape that had once been trees and grass and crops. Smoke rose from fires dotted around, some large enough to be buildings, some more likely vehicles.

Finally, right at the edge of what she could see, and getting less clear by the moment, she could see a dark dish, the size of a cruise liner, sitting amongst the charcoaled countryside. Rising from this, in a tree-trunk of light which must have been many yards wide was a beam of green light. It lit the charred land below it with a sickly hue that made her stomach lurch.

Where it reached into the sky, fresh clouds were boiling, thick and black, and from there they spread out at a frightening speed. She turned and looked, just in time to see the last of the blue vanish over the other horizon as the clouds finally covered everything in sight.

"What are they-?" Sam asked.

"Darkness," was Nicola's response. "They need darkness."

As if summoned by her words, a screaming growl sounded from the valley behind them.

Thirty-seven

James was supposed to be leading the group, but once he'd told Alan and Andy that it was nothing more than a straight road leading to the village, they took the responsibility from him. He was grateful.

Alan and Charlotte walked at the front, just ahead of James. Debbie and Ryan came behind, Debbie pushing Heidi's chair. Behind them were Bert and Doreen, and finally Andy and Sandra bringing up the rear.

Bert hadn't slept well in the cellar - God, none of them had – but he was certainly feeling his age today. He and Doreen, despite their many walks around the area, leaned on each other as they walked. She groaned and stumbled occasionally, and he wrapped his arm more securely around her to help her take her weight off her feet.

Eventually, he had to ask, "How far is this place, then, lad?"

The group paused as the sound of his voice caused Alan and James to look back. "Not far. About a mile," said James.

"Can you manage, love?" Bert asked his wife. She nodded and they hobbled on.

The road wound through the green countryside. Occasionally there were places where the hedge had been ripped away by the passage of... well, of *them*. Through some of the gaps they could sometimes see trampled crops.

Other times it was slaughtered livestock.

They rounded one bend, and again the group came to a halt. There was something in the road. Bert helped his wife to sit for a moment on the verge and walked up to the front. It was a body. That is to say, it was the remains of a person, but there was no head. The ragged flesh of the neck suggested that something had finally bitten off too much. James was shaking and Charlotte was holding him. Bert had noticed, even last night, that she seemed to have adopted the boy.

Bert helped Alan to lift the body to the side of the road. From the looks of it the corpse had once been a middle-aged man. They didn't know what else they could do. They were certainly in no position to carry the body with them until they could find somewhere more 'respectful' than an unkempt grass bank. Mind you, Bert mused, this would hardly be the last unburied body that would come out of all this when the dust settled.

He was sure that the dust *would* settle. An eternal optimist at heart, he firmly believed that whatever madness had gripped the country this time would blow over, just like all the others. Hadn't he outlived the craze for them jackets with big shoulders, and him in just his donkey jacket? Hadn't he seen fad after craze after recession after crisis come and go? This might be slightly different, but he was a firm believer that whatever happened, it all returned to normal again. Hell, look at the wars. They'd been the worst things in the world, but now look. There were youngsters who had no real idea of what had happened, why it had happened, and who wouldn't care anyway if you went and told them.

Having moved the body and folded the arms in as restful

a pose as a headless corpse could adopt, Bert scouted about for the head, but there was no sign of it.

In the end there was nothing more they could do for it, so he walked back to where Doreen was still sitting. He felt that somehow he should have done more, but short of being there to stop those damn things from attacking the poor man in the first place he didn't know what it could have been.

Doreen looked worse than when he left her, and although he heaved, and Andy helped, they couldn't get her back onto her feet. "I'm sorry, lads. It's me hip. It just won't take no more." She looked up into Bert's eyes and he could see the fear there. "You better just leave me here," she told him. "You can't stay."

Bert fixed her with a gaze that communicated how much he loved her, how much he needed her, and all the other things that had never needed to be said after their 42 years of marriage.

"Like fuck we will!" he replied, then turned to the group. "Right, then. We need some way of carrying my missus with us. I'm not leaving her. Any ideas?"

He looked from face to face, sure that something would be worked out. Something was *always* worked out. He waited, and knew it would come. And it did.

"Oh, God!" It came from James. "I'm so stupid!" He actually slapped his forehead in his moment of realisation. He turned to Alan and shouted, "Come on, I need your help!" into his face. Then he ran off back the way they had come. Alan, after a moment's surprise and a confirmation nod from Charlotte, ran after him.

They all waited, wondering what had possessed the boy, but after no more than 10 minutes, they knew. They heard it before they saw it. It was the unmistakeable clip and clop of a horse's hooves on the road. Moments later it came round the corner: a large dray-horse pulling an old fashioned milk-wagon. James was sitting on the board at the front, holding the reins with a look of contentment on his face which made him look much younger even than his 17 years. Alan stood behind him in the cart, looking nonplussed.

"It's our neighbour's!" James called as he came into view. "They keep Buster in a stable and I just knew that he would have been all right. They use this sometimes for delivering the organic milk and for the summer fetes and things like that. Will this do?"

This last was addressed to Bert who, like the boy, was grinning wide enough to split his cheeks. "Oh yes, lad. It'll do alright. It'll do just fine!"

James drew the milk wagon to a halt just in front of where Doreen was sitting. Alan jumped down and between him and Andy, they hoisted Doreen up into the back. They propped her against the side with some sacking to soften it for her. Bert was then pulled up by his arms and moved to sit out of the way, with Doreen, while Heidi was lifted up, still in her chair, and the others all followed.

Once loaded, Alan pulled up the tailgate to stop them falling out, and with a 'chook' noise and a flick of the reins, James set the cart into motion once more.

The horse had gone barely four or five steps when the sky started to darken overhead. Bert looked up and his heart sank as he watched thunderheads boil from the west and blot out the blue.

Thirty-eight

The horse slowed as the light dimmed, and James let it. He, like the others, was staring upwards. His brain was still numb from the events of the last day, but if he could have plucked out a single coherent thought it would have been, *Oh God, what now?!*

They all sat for a moment, watching the fine summer's day replaced with dark wintery clouds, but then Alan touched his arm and he jumped.

"Go," said Alan. "I don't know what it is, but I doubt it's anything good. So, go! Drive! We need to get to wherever we're going as soon as possible."

James nodded and lowered his head to his task. He flicked the reins and Buster started his slow plod once more. The horse was never going to win any races, but it was at least faster than walking. And managing the horse gave him something to think about; something to take his mind off everything else. It was a familiar action: he had grown up helping the Henderson's with the horse and had been driving on their rounds with them since he was 12. It was an anchor which was helping him to stay on the ground when all he wanted to do was float away.

The day grew darker and darker, so that, even though it was the clouds which were covering them, it felt as though they were heading into onrushing darkness. It didn't matter to James, though. He knew these lanes well, and when necessary he had driven the horse in the dark to deliver the milk. Sometimes he would have Mr Henderson with him, but sometimes, especially after Mr Henderson had his heart-attack, he had driven these dark lanes with his dad. James fixed on that image, of the large man sitting by his side, correcting his technique on the reins when necessary, and used it to blot from his mind the image of the melting mass that had been his dad's ending.

The road twisted and turned and James gave Buster such guidance as he needed. Not much was necessary, if he was honest. Buster had followed this route even more times than James. If left to his own devices, he would probably have wandered the route on his own.

It was full twilight when they reached the town, and James was surprised to see the first buildings loom out of the gloom. Yes, he had done this journey in the dark, but he had always been welcomed by the streetlights and nightlights in some of the houses. But, the power was out, of course, and there were no lights, just large blank boxes lining the road.

The sound of Buster's hooves echoed off the buildings as they paced between them. No other sound came from the town.

"Where do you think, then, lad?" Bert asked from the back of the wagon. "The Farrier?" he asked, referring to the village pub.

James shook his head. "No, too many doors, too many windows. I was thinking The Hut."

Bert nodded approval. "Good thinking, lad."

Alan looked from one to the other, peering through the darkness to see their faces. "The Hut? What's that?"

"You never been to Little Shotterling, Alan?" asked Bert.

"Well, yeah, through it, but never, you know, to stay. So what's 'The Hut'?"

It was James who replied. "It's the scout hut. It has a kitchen with water and plates and that, and a couple of toilets."

"Okay, so far so good. But why there in particular?"

"Well, a couple of years ago there were kids throwing stones and breaking windows and that, when it was empty. So they bricked up most of the windows, covered the rest with thick wire, and put some really thick doors on it. It's a mini-fortress."

Alan nodded, he could see the thinking behind it now. "Okay, let's go."

"Erm..." said Bert from the back of the cart. "We might have a problem."

James looked back over his shoulder to where Bert was pointing. It was hard to see through the gloom, but he didn't really need to see to guess what it was.

The noise of Buster's hooves had done a good job of broadcasting their presence as well as masking the approach of unwelcome visitors. But now he could hear the inexorable stamp of feet, and a low growling, snarling coming from behind them.

Buster heard it too, and James felt the reins jerk in his hands as the horse tossed his head in distress. The cart jerked as Buster found a turn of speed which James had never seen from him before. They moved from a walking speed up to a slow trot. James tugged to try and control the horse, but the beast was just too big, too heavy and too disconcerted to pay attention.

Whatever speed the horse had found, however, wasn't going to be enough to outrun those creatures. He heard a grunt and the sound of metal on flesh, and glanced back long enough to see Andy standing at the rear of the cart, Bert hanging onto the back of his jacket to keep him balanced. Andy's feet were planted and he was just swinging back his golf club into a 'batting' position over his shoulder. He had obviously just repelled a boarder.

Alan turned in his seat, placing his hand on James's shoulder, making to head back and help with the task. James thought it was probably a good idea. One man with a golf-club was only going to be able to do so much.

But then James fixed his eyes on the road ahead and raised his hand to grab Alan's sleeve. "Erm… Alan."

Alan looked down at him, one leg already hooked over the seat into the wagon. "What?"

James didn't say anything, just used his head to indicate ahead of them.

Alan turned and looked and saw what had caused James's mute state. The road ahead, where it widened out to pass around the green, was filled from edge to edge with zombies. They weren't moving, just standing and waiting. They didn't need to come to the wagon. Buster was taking them towards the wall of undead flesh at a canter.

Thirty-nine

They didn't pause. No-one needed to discuss what the noise meant. As soon as they heard the howl in the darkness, they knew they had to run. Nicola picked up the threshing blade which she had rescued from the pool of red goo which had once been Stan, and which she had dropped when she saw the splintered door of the shed. She still had the pack on her back.

She set off at a run and the others followed.

At first she didn't think about where she was running to. The important word was 'away': away from the noise approaching from the valley. Very soon, however, Dave was at her side. "Where are we going to go?" he asked her.

She thought for a moment. If Alyssa was anywhere, she was probably with the horde which was ascending towards them. She would be in their mix, adding her piping snarl to the massed sound. Nicola did not want to see that. And, if by some miracle, her girl was still alive, she would be somewhere other than down there. So, away from them was certainly the best bet. But where to? She could only think of one place, and she realised it was already where they were heading.

"The village," she panted as she ran. "The others might... have found shelter... and we might... be able to find them."

Dave nodded and she saw him glance back to check on

the others.

For all that he had let her down, he was turning out to be a good man. She felt, rather than saw, as he dropped back, and she risked a glance to see him helping Sam whose trainers were slipping off, despite the extra socks. He had his arm around her shoulder and she was kicking them off. Sam looked up and saw Nicola looking back. "I'll be better in socks. Used to run school cross country in bare feet! Like Zola Budd, you know?"

Nicola just nodded and kept going. It wasn't like they could stop for the girl to adjust her clothing, anyway.

At least it was downhill for this part, she thought. Gravity was their helper. Even as the thought passed through her mind, she caught her foot on a hussock of grass, the weight of her backpack pushed her centre of gravity up, and she fell forward, rolling even as she hit the ground. She carried on, unable to stop, sometimes with the pack beneath her, sometimes on top, rolling, skidding and falling down the hill.

She finally stopped, dazed and winded, once the ground started to level off. She knew she was lucky not to have hit her head on any rocks on the way down, but she felt like she had been battered. She lifted her head, looking around, trying to see where she was, and trying to force her protesting muscles to lift her from the floor. She had barely managed to focus when the others arrived at her side, their own momentum causing them to leap and gallop down the hill. Tony and Daz reached her at about the same time, Dan just behind them and Dave still monitoring Sam, the two of them coming down more slowly.

Barely slowing, the two men in front scooped her up onto her feet and carried her backwards a little way until they could control their flight long enough to set her down. Tony pulled on her arm to get her facing back in the right direction. His face asked a question and she nodded to answer it, telling him she was okay to carry on.

Dave and Sam arrived moments later, nearly colliding with the backs of the others, and then they were off again.

The ground had levelled off again, so it was easier to stay balanced, but harder to keep moving. Nicola was aware now of the weight of the pack on her back, and her knees and thighs hurt where they had slammed into the ground during her tumble.

She ran more slowly now, a slight limp in her stride. Tony and Daz, although capable of greater speed, stayed at her side. Part of her wanted to tell them not to worry and to just run, but the greater part was glad they were there in case she needed them. She had already been scared, but falling down the hill had only added to it.

Now they were back on the flat, and without the sun or the road to guide them, Nicola was no longer sure they were heading in the right direction. The haze in her head from the fall didn't help. She wanted to glance back in case seeing the hill would help her orientate herself, but she didn't dare in case she tripped again. She had to rely on Tony and Daz having some sense of where they were going.

She hated relying on others at any time, but now it seemed so much worse. She had grown used, in such a short time, to being the one in charge, the one who the others followed. But now she was the one that had to be led. She hated it.

They had reached the first real field – covered with low crops rather than ovine body parts - when the howl sounded behind them again. She could tell it was coming from the top of the hill and knew that now their attackers would have the advantage of gravity to help them catch up. She tried to go faster but her knee threatened to buckle. Tony moved closer to her, slid his hand round her back underneath the straps of the pack, and lifted.

With the weight no longer pulling on her, she found her legs were stronger than she had thought. She felt him lift and tug at the pack and she let her arms slip from it, only barely breaking stride as she did so. He swung it away from her and passed her the shotgun. He slipped it over one shoulder, then up onto his back, adjusting his stride to compensate. He reached out his hand and she passed the gun back to him.

As she ran, feeling so much lighter now, she glanced at him. She was still angry with him for what he had done to Sam, but she couldn't stop herself from feeling warm towards him too. Taking her pack was such a selfless and generous gesture, and she couldn't imagine the man who she had pulled from his car less than 24 hours earlier doing such a thing. He had changed so much, and for the better. She didn't know, couldn't know, how this craziness would end. But she thought it might just be the making of him.

It was a strange thought to have in the middle of this mad dash, but then again what wasn't strange about the things they were caught up in. Spaceships? Zombies? Giant robots? Laser beams that made clouds? In the midst of all that, thinking about how someone might be becoming a better person seemed positively liberating; like an oasis of normality in the madness.

Feeling stronger and more able, she risked a glance back. She tried to shout, but her voice caught in her throat.

Despite the dark she could make out the shapes flooding

down the hill. But that wasn't what had made her shout. The first two shapes – creatures that had once been men – had almost reached them.

She managed to cough out a, "Look out," but it was too late. They had launched themselves into the air, and one each landed on the backs of Sam and Dave. She tried to turn, to go back, but Tony grabbed her arm and pulled her along.

"Just... keep... running!"

Forty

Alan joined James in pulling at Buster's reins, but to no avail. The horse simply pulled back, then used his strong neck muscles to toss his head so hard that the reins were pulled from their hands. The shock of losing hold sent Alan, who had been standing, crashing back into the seat, nearly knocking James and himself to the road. But James managed to jam his leg into the side board and push back, keeping them both from falling into the path of the zombies.

They re-seated themselves, gazing forward impotently as the wagon neared the wall of zombies, then realised they needn't have worried. Buster was stopping for neither man nor zombie. He ploughed straight into the waiting group, trampling and kicking as though he knew they were the enemy. Others disappeared into the iron-rimmed wheels of the coach, causing it to jolt and bounce. James glanced back and saw, with relief, that the others had seen what was coming and had braced themselves. Andy had sat down again, and was helping Bert and Doreen weather the worst of this roller-coaster ride.

He looked back and saw that they were reaching the back of the crowd, which must have been ten deep. Buster had cut a swathe through them. However, doing so had slowed him somewhat and one zombie, fast enough to dodge the slower horse, leapt past him for the front of the wagon.

James recoiled in fear, but Alan didn't pause. He rose once more to his feet and swung the stout metal bar which had been his weapon of choice. James closed his eyes before the impact, but heard it hit with a dead, crunching thud. He opened his eyes and the zombie was gone. In fact, all the zombies were gone. The road was clear ahead of him.

Alan turned and jumped into the back of the wagon, and James heard more thumping and crunching. James didn't want to look, didn't want to see, but presumed the noise was Alan and Andy swinging their weapons of choice at zombies who had managed to gain purchase on the moving cart. With nothing to impede him, Buster was picking up speed again, and soon the noises stopped. James risked a glance back and saw the two men, standing straddle-legged in the wagon, sweating but grinning, patting each other on the back. Andy had large ragged scratches on his arm which were oozing blood, but otherwise the two seemed unhurt.

Then James was aware of a low moaning coming from beside the two men, and worried for a moment that a zombie had got past them. It wasn't a zombie, though, it was Bert cradling Doreen in his arms. She seemed to have fainted.

Then James saw the blood. It covered her head in a caul. No, it was worse than that. It was her head. A zombie must have flung its arms over the side of the wagon, grabbed her under the neck and ripped her head clean off when it fell back. What lay in Bert's lap as the old man keened, was the slowly draining headless corpse of his wife.

James leant over the side of the wagon and threw up. There wasn't much in his stomach so it was mainly burning acid. The world swam in front of him, not helped by the sight of the road passing under the wagon. He vomited again, and for a moment the world went black.

When he came back to his senses, the road was still rushing in front of his eyes, and a commotion was coming from the back of the wagon. He pulled himself upright and looked back. Bert was on his feet, Doreen's body lying where she had fallen, and Andy and Alan were holding his arms to prevent him from leaping from the back of the cart.

"You bastards! You fucking bastards! That was my wife! My wife! I'm going to kill every last one of you fuckers! Let go! For fuck's sake let me go!"

Despite his age he was still obviously strong, and managed to pull his right arm free from Andy's grip. His arm pistoned forward in sudden release, his whole body threatening to topple from the back, but Alan held him tight. As he came upright again, his loose arm whipped backwards and hit Andy in the stomach, knocking him onto his bottom with a whoosh of expelled breath. Bert turned his face up towards Alan, and despite the darkness, James could see the anger, the misery, and the pleading.

"Let me go!" He said, but his voice had lost some of its edge, some of its energy. "Please, Alan, mate, let me go. I need to go and… and… they… they…" He started to sob. He was still attempting to tug his left arm free, but only half his heart was in it now. Alan still didn't let him go. Instead, still balanced in the back of the fast-moving wagon, he pulled the old man against him, and held him tight, letting Bert's sobs bray into his shirt.

James watched for a moment, then turned back to the front, embarrassed at watching an old man cry, whatever the circumstances. He realised that Heidi was screaming too, just another noise in the mix, but he had seen that Debbie and Ryan had been okay, if shocked.

Looking ahead of their runaway wagon, James realised that Buster was starting to slow again. But there was no obstacle this time. Instead he saw their destination: The Hut. The horse, ignoring whatever was happening behind him, had brought them right to the door of their sanctuary.

As the horse slowed to a walk, James leapt down from the front of the wagon, his knee giving a twinge from where he had used it to brace himself against Alan's fall. He moved up alongside the horse and, matching his speed, grabbed for the reins. He moved ahead of the horse, leading him now instead of the other way around, and took the wagon up to the door of the Hut, shushing him to a halt.

"We're here," he shouted.

Alan looked over at him and nodded. Andy, who was now back on his feet, looked back down the street they had just travelled down. "They don't seem to be following," he said. "But let's be quick." He moved to open the tailgate of the wagon and started to help Alan lift Bert down.

James watched as Andy helped the broken form of Bert round towards him. "Don't leave her? You won't leave her, will yer? You'll bring her, yeah?" he was mumbling to the former chef.

"Don't worry, Bert. I'll get you in and then I'll get her myself. I promise."

"Good lad. Good lad. You'll get her. Yeah. You'll get her, won't yer? You won't leave her?"

Andy carried on reassuring him as they made their way to the door of The Hut. Meanwhile, Alan and Ryan were helping Debbie down, Heidi clutched in her arms.

"Erm…" a voice sounded behind him.

James turned. It was Andy, his hand on the door of the scout building. "Do you have a key?"

Forty-one

Tony only took three steps alongside Nicola, then he pushed her to keep her running, stopped and turned. Dan and Daz looked at him in surprise as he faced them, and tried to stop too. "No! Keep going! Get her to safety!" He flapped a hand at his shoulder to indicate Nicola. They looked confused for a moment, then saw him start to raise the shotgun to his right shoulder, nodded, and ran on.

He took a few steps back towards where Sam and Dave were lying. The zombies had pushed them over, but hadn't managed to get any purchase. Dave, flat on his back, was waving his pick-axe around, keeping them at bay. Tony glanced up at the horde which was still coming down the hill, then back to the scene in front of him. He steadied his feet, socked the stock of the gun into his shoulder, and took aim.

"Down!" he shouted. Dave dropped his arms and Sam made herself as flat as possible. The zombies did the opposite, his voice attracting their attention, making them pause and look up at him.

He pulled the triggers.

The blast was stronger than he expected, and the stock was not firmly seated enough, so it recoiled into his shoulder, knocking him back and numbing his arm. He tottered backwards but managed to stay on his feet, holding onto the gun with his left hand as his right dropped to his side. Finally stable on his feet again, he looked up to see what effect he'd had.

The creature which had been standing above Dave was now flat on its back behind him, its head missing. The other had lost an arm, and was staggering, but still growling and making moves towards the two prostrate humans., Bearing its teeth it made a lunge towards Sam, and Dave finally connected with the pickaxe, repeated the trick he had used on zombie-Stan, and piercing its head, this time ear to ear. The punch of it threw the zombie to the side, wrenching the axe from Dave's hand. It landed, motionless.

Seeing this, Tony all but leapt the last few steps. He dropped the gun and used his good left arm to drag Sam to her feet. Dave heaved himself up next to them. The pursuing zombie pack was racing towards them.

Tony stopped and grabbed the gun, Dave made a move to retrieve his axe, but Tony pressed the gun to his chest instead. "Here, take this." He flopped his right arm, which was starting to tingle and hurt, but still wouldn't respond. "I can't anyway. Now let's get the fuck out of here!"

They turned and ran after Nicola and the others, just ahead of the snarling pack of once-human creatures.

Tony's right arm was really hurting, and he cradled it in his left as he ran, every step jolting fresh shots of pain

On his right, Dave had cracked open the shotgun and emptied the two spent cartridges. He looked over at Tony. "More?"

Without thinking, Tony went to reach into the right hand pocket of his jacket where he had stowed a double handful of the ammunition. The arm obeyed him at last, but it was too painful and he let it drop and dangle again before scooping it up in his other one again.

Dave watched this and understood the problem. He moved closer to Tony and reached in to grab a pair of shells from Tony's pocket. The movement proved too awkward for them, though. He stumbled, catching his foot in the grass and pulling the two of them to the ground.

Tony instinctively flung out his arms to break his fall, the weight of the pack on his back making it feel much faster than normal. He screamed when his bad arm crumpled under his weight; a scream which was muffled when his face hit the grass a second later. He tried to roll onto his back but couldn't because of the pack and could only make it onto his side. He felt Dave's hand pull free of his jacket and the click-click-snap of the weapon being swiftly loaded and locked. It was obvious that Dave knew much more about guns than he did, and wondered why on earth he hadn't asked for someone who would be better placed to use it without hurting themselves than him. This thought was followed by the realisation that he could hear the drumbeat of running feet coming up to him through the earth to which his ear was pressing. They were coming.

He heard a scream – a battle-cry – from his right, followed by the loud booming discharge of one barrel and then the other. The sounds of bodies hitting the floor came up to him through the ground, but it was only two from a host.

He felt Dave's hand scrabbling for his pocket again, but it was too late. The zombies were on them.

Forty-two

They tried with their various implements to get into the Hut. Alan's metal bar was too thick, but Bert had brought a crow-bar which they were able, just, to get into the gap between the double-doors at the side of the Hut. Alan applied all his strength, and then leant his weight on the bar, but nothing happened. The immovable object didn't move and his force was more than resisted.

He tried again, at the hinges, but still nothing happened. "They must be metal doors and frames," he concluded, but kept trying anyway.

James alternated between watching his efforts, glancing to the side where Debbie was comforting Bert while Andy kept an eye on him to stop him trying again to do something stupid, and watching down the road for signs of pursuit. He didn't know why the zombie army hadn't come running after them, but then realised that trying to understand them was pointless. Who knew why they did anything when, in a sane world, they should simply have laid down and died? Ascribing motives to them was pointless. All he could do was wait and see.

Ryan was rolling the pushchair back and forth, soothing Heidi. Buster was munching the weeds which grew up in the grass at the side of the Hut. It all seemed so quiet and so normal, he couldn't believe what they had just been through. But there was no way he could enjoy it. He knew it was a break, a rest, a brief hiatus; nothing more. In a minute, or ten, or an hour, he knew that they would be running for their lives again, especially if they couldn't get into the Hut. He didn't know if he could face that, and felt sweat break out on his face. His hands started shaking and he turned, grabbed the crow-bar from a surprised Alan, and started to batter on the door.

"Open up! Open up! Open up!" He smashed the crow bar off the door over and over. It vibrated in his hand, and made his arm tingle painfully, but he didn't stop.

"Open up! Open u-." When the door suddenly opened, James was nearly as surprised as the young man who nearly got the crowbar in his face. The man stepped back to avoid the blow from the crowbar, and the door swung with him. Without stopping to think, James had his foot in, pushed the door, and was into the Hut.

He turned round, shouted, "We're in!" to the others, turned back and shrieked when he saw the gun barrel pointing into his face.

He put his hands up in the air, dropping the crowbar which bounced on the concrete step with a clang.

"Are you all safe?" asked the young man, who James now realised had stepped back, not just to avoid the crowbar, but to give himself room to swing his rifle up. James also noticed, even in his panicked condition, that the man was wearing an army uniform. Which explained the rifle, he thought, and almost laughed.

"Yes. Yes. We're fine. Not zombies, not aliens, nothing. Just humans. Ordinary humans who haven't been changed into anything, or bitten, or nothing. Don't shoot, we're like you, we're normal. We're just looking for somewhere to hide, somewhere safe. Don't shoot!"

The soldier had already lowered his rifle in the middle of James's verbal diarrhoea, but as James had squeezed his eyes shut, he didn't realise. He only stopped when he felt a hand on his shoulder. He shrieked again, but opened his eyes to see the soldier looking at him with a vaguely amused look his face.

"Come on. There's no way you're anything other than human. Let's get you all inside and lock the door again before something other comes along."

He pushed James past him and stepped out to tell the others to come in. James walked through the small lobby area and through a doorway into the room beyond. In a building with the windows bricked-up and the sky outside covered in thick clouds, James expected the room to be completely dark, but it was lit by the gentle light from dozens of candles set up along the cupboards which lined the room.

It looked like a shrine, or a church. Or maybe, he thought, it looked like what it was: part-cave, part-sanctuary.

The others crowded in behind him, marvelling with him at the fairy-tale nature of the scene. Heidi cooed something in baby talk, and Debbie pushed her further into the room. It was then that James noticed the other people. It had taken him a moment for his eyes to get used to the combination of bright and dark in the room, and he hadn't noticed the dark shapes which were huddled at the far end, looking up at them.

It was only when one of them stood that his eyes detected the movement and he realised there had to be thirty people already in the Hut; people who'd had the same idea as him.

The figure which stood looked too short to be an adult.

It stepped forward and some of the candle-light fell on its face, showing it to be a small girl, no more than six or seven.

"Mummy? Are you here? Is that you, Mummy?"

The soldier pushed past James and walked over to the girl. "Sorry, Alyssa. This group's mostly men. I don't think your mother's with them."

James heard the girl sob, and the soldier, his rifle still held in his left hand, bent and put his right arm around her shoulder. "Don't worry. I'm sure she's on her way. She'll be here soon."

Forty-three

Tony felt a dead weight land on him. Dead, but freakishly alive. Hands scrabbled at him, as the zombie climbed up him, clutching at clothes and the pack, hauling itself towards his neck. He tried to fight it off, but with only one arm it wasn't easy. He pushed and tried to swing a punch, but the zombie simply carried on moving. His head was craned around, and he saw the zombie's face appearing over his shoulder. Its hair was matted with blood, and one eye seemed to have popped and run down its cheek. Its skin was a waxy-white, but its teeth and mouth were stained-black: the colour of blood turned to the colour of death by the gloom.

As it got close enough, it reared up, ready to plunge its mouth down over the restricting band of the backpack strap, and Tony had enough time to be amazed that there was no panting, no smell of gory breath just an underlying growl as it prepared to bite. Its head went up and back and Tony tried one last push with his arm, but it wasn't enough to shift it. Although he didn't want to see, he stared into the thing's dead eye as it plunged towards him, deciding that if this was his last act, at least he could face it.

Forty-four

When she heard the double-shot, Nicola glanced back and saw Tony stagger. She nearly turned to go back, but saw him catch himself and then saw Dave and Sam on their feet again and running after her and the others. She turned back and carried on running.

She glanced back again after she heard two single shots, and saw that Dave now had the gun and seemed to be wrestling with Tony. The mass of zombies had made it down the hill and were closing on the others.

And then they went down: her Dave and Sam and Tony. She let out a wordless yell and turned back. She didn't know if Dan or Daz were with her, and she didn't care. She also didn't know if it was the sight of Dave in danger, or Tony, or even both of them, but she knew she had to help. There were so many of the zombies, it was hopeless really, but she couldn't just keep running and leave them to it. She's already done that at Tony's urging and it had been wrong. Damn, why did she just fold and do what other people told her?

All of this passed through her head as she ran back to her friends. It seemed like the whole pack of the undead had slowed to allow its lead members to feast. Three of them leapt, each one aimed at one of the fallen. Sam was closest to her, and Nicola ran up, and swung with her blade. It hit the zombie in the side of the head, splitting its skull, and it went over, still thrashing, still undead.

The creature was on Sam's far side, and Nicola's momentum was still carrying her forward. She took a step and was next to Tony, where his attacker was crawling over his body heading for his neck. She managed to stop this time, waited for the zombie to pause, which it did with its head held high, and aimed carefully. Her makeshift sword passed through what was left of its neck and sent its head soaring into the air.

She didn't wait to see it land, but turned back to finish off the one which had been attacking Sam, but Dan was already there, burying his pickaxe in the zombie's head with one hand, and pulling Sam to her feet with the other. She looked the other way and saw Daz standing over Dave, swinging his sledgehammer from side to side, knocking away zombie after zombie. Most of them got straight back up. But some of them caught a skull-crushing blow to the head and stayed down.

There was a click, and Nicola realised why it was that Dave had still been on the ground. She saw him raise the shotgun against his shoulder, and with two swift shots remove the heads of two zombies.

Between these shots and Daz's hammer-swinging, enough of a gap had been made for the two of them to scramble back from the still sizable horde approaching them. Some residual cunning must have remained in the zombie's brains, as they no longer charged, but were approaching more cautiously. Daz helped Dave to his feet and Nicola realised that the only one still on the floor was Tony, turned-turtle beneath the weight of a headless zombie. She put her foot on the corpse and pushed it off him, then reached down and tried to pull him to his feet.

She realised he could only use one arm, and the effort of trying to lift him and his pack was too much. He nearly pulled her down with him.

She tried again, and then Dan and Sam reached her from one side, and Dave and Daz from the other, between them they hoisted Tony from the floor and placed him on his feet.

She wondered if they should turn and run again, but no-one made any move to do so.

This, it would seem, was the place they would stop running. This was where they would take their stand.

Tony, Dan, and Daz allowed their packs to drop to the floor. Tony passed his whole jacket, with its pockets-full of shotgun shells, to Dave. Then finding himself weaponless, Tony reached into the pack at his feet and found a long screwdriver.

And so each of them, armed with a range of makeshift weapons – and the one gun which Dave was already loading again – planted their feet in the dirt of an anonymous field, under a blackened sky, and waited for the enemy to attack.

Forty-five

There were three soldiers in the Hut, the rest, apart from Alyssa, were villagers who had had the same idea of using the unusually fortified scout hut as a refuge from the madness.

The newcomers made themselves as comfortable as they could on the wooden floor of the hut and listened while Scott, the solder who had let them in, told them what had happened.

"We were being transported in by helicopter to engage the hostiles when they got us first. There were twelve of us, including the pilots, but only six of us survived. When the…" he paused, unable to believe what was about to come out of his mouth, "… when the *aliens* hit us with their beams, they split the helicopter. We were at the back and fell out. We weren't that high up and landed on soft grass, so we were okay. The rest of the helicopter, with everyone in it, went down and exploded. We were lucky to escape.

"Our first thought was to head to the LZ on foot, but before we could, there was a blast and everything between us and the target was vaporised. We were blown into a ditch by the blast, and the ditch saved us. The fire-front rolled right over the top of us. Still, only four of us made it. Billy and Gobbo weren't close enough to be carried as far as the ditch. They burned up right in front of me."

He was telling the story in a low, matter of fact voice. It was obvious he had told it already, but it was still affecting him.

"The trees above the ditch started burning and flaming branches started to drop on us. We had to run for it, through the flames. The other side was the road. We found a burning truck and cars, but no people. They had all been abandoned. We presumed the people had fled into the woods, so we followed, but we didn't find any."

James heard Andy say something to Alan, and then Alan spoke up. "We met some of them. We met people who were there. One saw your helicopter go down and then the truck flew over onto the road. Was it your helicopter crash that sent it over, do you think?"

Scott nodded. "Probably."

"They headed into the woods, but then they got split up. One of them was her mother, I think." He turned to Alyssa. "Is your mummy called Nicola, honey?" he asked her and she nodded. Alan looked back at Scott. "They went looking for her. In some shed on a hill?"

Scott nodded. "Yes, that's where we found her. We rescued her before some of those zombie things could get to her."

"What are they?" James was surprised to realise that it was him who had asked the question.

"They're zombies, as far as I can tell. You know, the living dead and all that crap? *They* make them and then it spreads in the bite from creature to creature. They melt in the sun and you can stop them by smashing their heads in or chopping them off. That's all I know, really."

"The aliens made them?" Alan asked, and James saw Scott wince at the word. Something in his rational, army training just seemed to rebel at the idea.

"Yes, we saw them, we think.

"After we crossed the road and went through the woods, we came out into fields. We kept going in the hope of seeing a farm or a village. It didn't take long before we did see a farm, but before we could get there, we saw something else.

He paused and looked at the newcomers with a fixed stare. "What I'm going to say may sound crazy, but you have to believe me, okay?"

They all nodded, and James wondered what could be crazier than everything he had seen and heard so far in the last day.

"The..." Scott still obviously found it hard to say the word 'aliens', "...the attackers have ships – *spaceships* – which drop legs and become giant robot spiders which can walk around the countryside."

He waited for the stunned reaction that this comment had brought before, but all he got was nods. "Tell us something we don't know," said Bert, softly.

"Two of them demolished my pub," Alan filled in.

"Oh, I see." Scott even sounded a little disappointed at having his thunder stolen and James could suddenly see this young soldier as an old man, telling this story to wide-eyed grandchildren. If they all survived, that was.

"Well, one of them came across in front of us. It was headed straight for a man who had come out from the farm. For such big things they're amazingly quiet and fast. It was on him before we could shout. One of those legs just seemed to scoop him up in to the machine. Seconds later it pulled him back out in a shower of blood and dropped him, from what we could see, near the farmhouse. We ran, but when we got there, no-one was there. There was just a puddle of red on the carpet in the kitchen. We called, and walked around the farm, but we couldn't see what had happened.

"We worked out after that the puddle must have been what was left of the man we saw. The aliens had taken him in - bitten him themselves, maybe, we're not sure – and let him out to spread the infection. We think that's their plan to get rid of us, let us do it ourselves. Now they've blocked the sun it should be easy. Even a short exposure to the sun kills them. He must have gone in and melted in there."

"That was my dad," James said quietly. He then told his story, again, of what had happened to his dad and how he had hidden in the barn. Even as he was saying the words was aware that his voice held the same monotone as he had heard in Scott's.

When he finished, everyone was quietfor a moment, then Scott said, "That would explain what we found. When we got to the farm we must have just missed you, and your mum must have moved deeper into the house. After we found the… your father, we didn't really look further. We just called out and when we got no response we carried on.

"When night came we were near another farm, and that's when we saw what it really was we were facing. There were only three of them, all with their necks torn, but one of them was just a kid." He took a deep breath and shuddered.

"The kid ripped out Teddy's throat before we knew what was happening. They turned on us and we shot them. Five minutes later we had to shoot Teddy too." He stopped talking and everyone was silent for a moment.

One of the other soldiers picked up the story. James thought his name was Bolly, but he wasn't sure. Was that even a name? "We didn't want to carry on after that. It was dark, and we just had no real idea what was going on. They didn't brief us before they sent us in. Just that there had been an 'invasion'-" He almost spat the words, his scorn much deeper and more angry than Scott's bewilderment. "- and that we were being sent in to fight. We'd lost our way and our will. We sat and we talked and we tried to work it out. And then it was full dark. We already knew, from trying at the first farmhouse, that some kind of EMP had knocked out the power to anything useful, but we found some firewood and made a fire. It was a warm night, and it was kind of pleasant.

"Until *they* came."

"I guess the light and the smell of smoke drew them," Scott continued with the story. "There must have been forty of them. We shot some, but they kept coming, and we hadn't expected them. Our clips were in our bags, so we couldn't reload. We ended up in a barn, barricaded in. It was all we could do.

"They kept us there for hours, battering on the door, but we had pushed a tractor against it, and there was no way they were coming in. We just had to wait for them to leave."

Bolly continued, "Eventually they did, and when it had been quiet for a little while, we moved the tractor back and looked out. We could see a trail where they had headed out into the fields. We'd reloaded, and stashed our extra clips in our belt, and we thought that if we came up behind them, we could take most of them before they could turn on us.

"When we caught up with them, they were breaking into a shed and we could hear screaming. They were tearing the door into matchsticks with their hands and didn't care when they ripped off flesh or fingers. We took aim and shot a few of them in the heads, and the others turned and fled. They ran off the side, away from us. We didn't know what we had done to scare them so badly. Only hours before they hadn't seemed to care about our guns or the possibility of being shot. But only ten minutes later the sun came up, and we realised that they had known, somehow, and had run off to hide."

"We'd found Alyssa, by then," Scott carried on with this game of story-tag that he and his comrade had developed. "She'd been the one in the shed. I think if we'd been just one minute later, they would have got her. The door was almost gone: just so much kindling. We barely touched what was left and it collapsed. The girl was cowering in the back, but we eventually calmed her down."

"We brought her with us," – Bolly again – "and headed down the hill away from the farm, in the opposite direction from where the zombies had gone. There didn't seem to be any point following them, and from the hill we could see nothing but farms in that direction. Deek-" he indicated the third soldier who had said nothing so far, "-had a pair of field glasses in his kit and he said he could see a village over here, so we came this way.

"We reached the village just a few hours ago. We met all these people." He waved a hand around at the assembled group, none of whom had engaged in the story-telling, and to James they all looked in shock. "They were just emerging from cellars and garages, where they'd been hiding from their undead friends and loved ones all night. They were all heading here, the place that would be easiest to lock and defend. Some of them had made it here last night, and they let us in. And we've been here ever since."

With the story told, he fell silent. Scott didn't have

anything else to add, he just looked down between his crossed legs and rolled his rifle along his thighs.

"So," asked Alan, "what now?"

Scott looked up, and James could see in his expression that this was a question that he didn't want to answer. He took a deep breath. "Well, until the sun went, we were planning on scouting for food, but we can't do that now, not enough ammunition. So, when our food runs out, we'll last a while, as long as the water's still working. But-," he shrugged, "if nothing happens and no-one stops those things, I'm guessing we either have to try and break out of here and find a stocked shelter, or we simply wait to die in here."

The silence following this bald assessment was followed by a loud banging on the metal doors which reverberated through the building.

"Or maybe we won't have to wait."

Forty-six

The cautious advance of the zombies didn't last long once they saw that their prey was no longer running away. As they all reached the flat of the field, they ran, loping over the ground, some even dropping to all fours. The leader of the pack sprang straight at Nicola who was standing in the middle of the group of humans. She stepped back and started to swing her blade, but her foot sank into a depression and her arms went out wide as she struggled to stay upright. Her neck and chest were exposed, offered, to the zombie's attack.

Tony didn't even think, he just raised the hand with the screwdriver clutched in it directly in front of Nicola. The zombie impaled itself on the tool as it entered through the eye-socket. Tony couldn't stop the creature's flight. The screwdriver was torn from his hand and the zombie still collided with Nicola, knocking her back.

The breath flew from her in a whoosh as her back hit the ground, but still she rolled, dislodging the now-still body of the zombie from her, and scrambled to her knees, blade still clutched in her hand, trying to drag air into her lungs. Tony watched this, and wasn't aware of the creature which had used his distraction to launch itself at his neck. The first thing he knew was when the shotgun discharged close enough to his face for him to feel the singe of the blast on his skin and his right ear to start ringing with deafness. He turned in shock and saw the headless corpse of a zombie flying backwards, seemingly propelled by a cloud of blood and brains. He nodded his thanks to Dave, who took a brief moment only to nod back before turning the second barrel on another approaching attacker.

Beyond him, Tony could see Dan and Daz swinging with their weapons, knocking zombies to the ground on either side of them. While the attack on Nicola had driven her and Tony backwards, Dan and Daz had advanced into the oncoming crowd, dealing blows to left and right. Some of their blows were enough to kill the creatures, but many only stopped their progress and the undead things lurched back to their feet and resumed their frenzy. Sam was standing behind the two men, and Tony realised for the first time – how could he not have noticed? – that she had no weapon of her own. He hadn't thought to check when they left the farm, but had been too caught up in what Nicola had been doing with Dave. How could he be so utterly thoughtless? He cursed under his breath, stooped to pull his screwdriver from the dead thing at his feet, and saw Nicola already back on her feet and ready to face the oncoming horde. Dave's shotgun blasts had caused some of them to pause, and they had turned their attention to the two men and Sam. Finding that they were enclosed in an area of calm, Tony led Nicola and Dave towards the others, to aid them in their fight and their protection of Sam.

He had only taken the first step when it happened. A zombie broke from the circumference of the undead which had formed just outside the radius of their swing, and flung itself at Daz's side as the momentum of his sledgehammer left him exposed. The zombie didn't gain a hold, but its force was enough to knock him off-balance, colliding with

Dan, and the two of them tumbled to the floor.

Sam was frozen, watching as the defence which had kept her safe crumbled. Tony could do nothing but watch as one of the undead monsters launched itself at her and bore her to the ground.

Forty-seven

"They're on the roof!"

The attack had started at the front door, but it had soon become clear from the noises coming from outside that the entire Hut was surrounded. It seemed that, despite taking their time, the crowd which they had met on the road had followed them and were now determined to break inside their protective shell to find the tasty, soft centre.

James wondered, even as the noises started to come from above and Alan shouted the obvious conclusion, if Buster was okay. That should have been the last of his worries, he knew, but he couldn't help but speculate.

The sounds from above grew louder as more and more of the creatures found that the walls were too sturdy to be broken, but provided sufficient handholds for climbing.

With the start of the attack, everyone had risen to their feet, and stared around. Scott and the other soldiers had moved from the main room to the vestibule, to repel any zombies which managed to break through the door. The rest had stood, impotently, whatever weapons they had managed to find clutched loosely in their hands, and waited.

"Anyone know what the roof is made of?" asked Alan, looking around. In the candlelight, James could see all faces upturned, listening to the progress of footsteps across the flat surface above them. No-one looked down, but one or two slowly shook their heads.

The silence of their response was broken by a loud tearing noise from directly above the group, and one or two of the waiting survivors let out short screams.

The tearing, like the sound of sellotape being pulled from a dispenser, continued, inexorably, and James had an image of gravel covered tar-paper being ripped and shredded. It stopped to be replaced by thumping and banging, and the sound of growling.

James himself jumped as he felt something touch his hand, and looked down to see Alyssa looking up at him as she slipped her hand into his. She had moved away from Debbie, whom she had attached herself to as soon as the mother had arrived, and for some reason sought comfort from him. He clutched her hand in his and resumed his upwards stare.

It was hard to make out in the gloom, but James thought he saw the roof start to shudder under the combined blows. Then, with a crack, he knew that they were having success. Dust dropped into his eyes where the plaster on the ceiling had splinted, and he bent his head, blinking away tears.

When he looked back up, it was in time to see the ceiling start to fall away in chunks. Plaster and concrete were falling into the room, yet still no-one moved. They were frozen, unable to do anything more than wait.

With another loud bang, a larger part of the ceiling fell away, and James was able to see a small patch of the gloomy sky which lowered above the Hut. It was obscured by grasping, groping hands, then reappeared, larger and stayed visible, steadily growing, as the creatures on the roof tore away the concrete with their bare hands.

Still no-one moved, they simply watched and waited.

As soon as the hole was large enough, the rain of

concrete and plaster stopped, and instead a body fell through into the Hut, screaming and spitting.

It hit the floor, its legs buckling under it, and despite the stasis which had seemed to hold them all, Andy didn't hesitate. He stepped forward and whipped his golf-club up under the jaw of the sprawled zombie, ripping it clean off. Alan, barely a step behind him, clubbed it across the back of the head with his iron bar, collapsing both skull and zombie in one blow.

Despite their speed of response, in the time it had taken them to despatch the first creature, three more had dropped through the still-widening hole in the roof into the hall of the hut. James could hear the booted feet of the solders running through from their watch of the front door, but he realised they were going to be too late as one of the zombies, turned, fixed its bloody and crazed eyes on him, and prepared to leap. He shoved Alyssa behind him and prepared to do what he could to protect her. He told himself to at least keep his eyes open.

The zombie launched itself, and even as it did, the floor bucked, sending it off course. James stumbled back as, with a roar of protesting earth, the Hut shifted beneath him. He collided with Alyssa and the two of them fell to the floor. He rolled off her, trying to make sure she was okay, and watched as the zombie turned from where it landed at his side and aimed its drooling jaws at him.

Despite his promise to himself, he closed his eyes as he waited to die.

Forty-eight

The zombies ignored Dan and Daz, who even as they fell were still swinging with their weapons in an attempt to impede their sudden progress. But with them down on their knees, it was much easier for the zombies to move in from the sides. Sam's flailing form disappeared under the mass of attacking undead.

Tony felt like a mime walking against the wind. Even as he pushed his legs forward, he didn't seem to be getting any closer. He saw Sam's hand appear above mass of bodies, and then disappear, sucked down and out of sight.

Another step finally made, Tony felt the world tilt around him and the floor shift under his feet. The roar of an explosion filled his one still-working ear, and light – so very bright after the gloom – lit the landscape in a sudden burst. He staggered to one knee, but the momentum of his run still brought his other leg through, dragging over the grass. He thrust his weight through that leg and came back to his feet, still moving, but only slowly realising that he could now see clearly.

He glanced upwards, not breaking stride and saw the clouds which had closed over their heads, breaking, wisping, disappearing into mist, and then gone. He looked back down and watched as, with time-lapse speed, the pile of zombies covering Sam melted away into so much red jelly, leaving her covered in their glistening scarlet.

As though a spell was broken, he felt speed return to his world and he was, in moments, at her side. He threw himself down next to her, his knees soaking in the mess which had been the attacking creatures, and started to wipe their residue from her face, praying for her eyes to open and for her lips to part in a relieved smile. Surely there hadn't been time, surely she would be okay.

Even through his closed lids, James could see the sudden light which poured through the hole in the roof. He felt warm wetness splash over his face, and then, nothing.

He squinted his eyes open into the sudden brightness and saw the thick beam of sunlight - made tangible by the candle-smoke – which shone down into the centre of the room. The light which lit the Hut was tinged scarlet by the pool of red which the sunlight hit, the pool which had been the creature that had melted even as it leapt at him.

He looked across the pillar of sunshine and saw Alan push another of the attackers into the light where it joined its companion in its puddle.

The third had made for the door, but the loud rifle shot which now sounded across the room as it met the returning soldiers ended its life too.

James waited, but nothing happened.

Everything was still, everyone was silent.

Nicola was just behind Tony, but when the earth shook and the light hit, she stopped. She watched as the attack literally melted away, and as Tony slid to the ground next to Sam. The girl was still, even as Tony wiped the remains of the zombies from her face, giving no reaction, making no protest.

She walked slowly up behind him, and the others, still shocked at the suddenness of their reprieve, nevertheless also gathered around.

They watched as Tony placed his hands on Sam's shoulders and shook her gently. "Come on, Sam, Come on. It's over." He glanced around as if to confirm for her that what he said was the truth. "They've gone. The sun's out. We're okay. Come on. Wake up. It's okay now, they've gone."

He let go of her shoulders and patted her face, but she didn't wake, even though he continued his entreaties. His patting caused her head to move to the side, and Nicola saw the gaping space where the side of her neck had been. She stepped up and placed her hand on Tony's shoulder, wanting to stop him, wanting to tell him that the girl was gone, but unable to make herself speak the words.

He carried on trying to rouse her, a combination of pleading words – slowly becoming more incoherent as sobs overtook him – shakes and pats. Sam didn't respond. She couldn't.

Words finally failing him, Tony carried on trying to wake her, but as he moved from her face to her shoulders once more, his fingers sank into her shoulders as whatever it was that turned a dead human into a zombie took hold of her. He expected her eyes to snap open showing whites stained with blood, and her lips to part in a snarling scream, but nothing like that happened. She simply melted away in his hands.

Tony shrieked, his head back, tendons standing out on his neck, as she melted down into the mire of her attackers. His cry became a wail, and Nicola dropped down next to him, ignoring the way her knees tried to recoil from the wetness that immediately soaked her jeans. She pulled him against her and held him while he screamed out his terror and loss.

Forty-nine

Scott insisted that he and his colleagues be the first to leave the Hut. They emerged, rifles at the ready, but there was nothing to shoot other than the red pool which glistened in the revealed midday sun. As they stepped out, a noise made them turn in alarm, but they managed to stop themselves before they shot Buster, who was wandering round the side of the Hut looking for clean grass to crop.

They shouted the all clear, and the refugees emerged. Alan and Andy assisted Bert, who kept mumbling that if only Doreen could have held on for a little longer it would all have been over.

James, leading Alyssa, was one of the last to leave the building, so was able to witness the moment the power came back on. The lights in the vestibule of the Hut flashed once, making him cry out and Alyssa clutch him, and then they came to life again and this time stayed lit. They seemed dim in comparison to the sunlight both outside and pouring through the hole in the main hall's roof, but their shining couldn't have felt sweeter to James.

They also lifted Alyssa's spirits, and she pulled away from James, singing, "The lights are on, the lights are on," and tugged people to come and see.

Despite the obvious signs of carnage, destruction and loss, there was a feeling of happiness and celebration in the group, and many of them acquiesced to Alyssa, following her to peer in at the simple strip lights which lit the entrance to the Hut.

No-one seemed in a hurry to get home. James watched them and wondered about that. He guessed it was the same thing he was feeling. Going home would remind them of what they had lost and what had happened. Staying here, in the sunshine outside the Hut, they could pretend that it was some other kind of gathering, a fete, a jumble sale, something. And maybe, now that the power was working again, someone would come and put everything else right. Maybe, if they waited, everything would just go back to normal.

James wandered a little way down the road, trying to imagine the darkness and the mad race through ranks of zombies. It all seemed like a dream now. But, in the distance, he could see a sign of reality. A thick column of dark smoke rose on the horizon, spreading out into a plateau of darkness. He turned on the spot, noticing a few others from the group had joined him and were likewise staring into the distance. He counted three more smoke columns and in his mind's eye saw many, many more of them sprouting all over the country; all over the world, maybe.

He was still standing, lost in thought, when he heard a shout from down the lane. He refocused on the immediate and saw a small band approaching. It only took a moment to recognise Nicola, Tony, Dave, Dan and Daz. He looked past them but couldn't see Sam.

As they reached him, he opened his mouth to ask, but Nicola shook her head and he closed it again. He looked around at their faces, at Tony's face, and saw his answer written there. Another one had fallen. Another lost, another gone. James felt, for perhaps the first time, the weight of his own losses. They threatened to overcome him, but then Nicola had let out a cry and run past him towards the Hut. Startled, James turned to watch her. As she ran towards the group still gathered at the Hut, he saw the small figure of Alyssa run towards her in turn.

As James watched, mother and daughter met in the middle of the street, and suddenly nothing else mattered. Nicola swept her daughter up into a hug and turned around and around with her in his arms. They were both talking and crying, their two voices mixed together in incomprehensible sobs and protestations of love and prayers of thanks. James knew that his sadness and loss would probably never leave him, and would revisit him in a thousand different ways to come, but in this one moment of reconnection he knew that despite the columns of rising smoke, life would go on.

Tearing his gaze away from Nicola, James glanced back at Tony, and saw tears running from his eyes unchecked. He could see hurt and loss in the man's eyes, but also a reflection of his own feelings. In amongst the pain he could see possibilities. Tony's eyes met James's, and the two shared a fractured smile. James realised that he too was crying.

The moment was broken by the sound of engines. Two army trucks came slowly into the village, and stopped by the Hut. Scott and his colleagues walked up and started talking with the important looking passenger in the front seat of the lead truck. With the return of power, however that had happened, Scott must have been able to radio in for reinforcements, and here they were. The hope of the villagers had been realised.

Maybe, he thought, just maybe it would all be all right.

Ignoring the arrival of the army, Nicola came back towards James and Tony, with Alyssa holding tight to her hand. Tony stepped forward and hugged Nicola, and then bent down to hug Alyssa too.

As he straightened up again, James heard a familiar electronic chirping sound which seemed strange and alien after just twenty four hours silence. Tony reached into his pocket and pulled out a mobile phone. He glanced at the screen, pressed a button with his thumb. He moved to take the phone in both hands in the familiar 'text-typing' grip, then stopped. He looked up at Nicola, around at the others, then back down at the phone. He shrugged and a small smile crossed his lips. He turned and threw the phone over the hedge and into the field. Then, taking Nicola's hand, and with James and the others following, he headed towards the trucks and whatever was going to happen next.

Epilogue

The alien invasion lasted a bare twenty-four hours in the end. If anyone ever actually knew where they came from, it was never made public. What was revealed was that it started with the unannounced arrival of a base-ship in orbit on the late morning of the first day. It quickly deployed smaller ships which travelled round the globe and attacked every military base on the planet simultaneously. This was just a way for them to land their ships in strategic locations and link them with a standing wave of some kind which acted to disable any electrical or electronic devices except those in their shielded ships and walkers.

It would seem, mused many commentators, that their goal was to wipe out the human race, but to leave as much of the infrastructure intact and operational as possible, by temporarily disabling it rather than destroying it. At the same time, they used the walkers to spread their virus, the 'zombie plague' as it became known. No-one who was scooped into the walkers was able to tell what had happened there. But the presumption was that the aliens passed on the plague through their bite, the action which the zombies used to propagate it further.

Experts calculated that, unchecked, the exponential spread of the virus would have consumed the whole human race in less than three days. Then, all the aliens would have had to do would have been take down their blanket of cloud and wait for the sun to wipe the earth clean.

With all electronics and electrics disabled, no realistic defence against the invasion could be mounted, nor co-ordinated. But words had already been sent to the right places.

At the moment of the arrival of the base-ship, instructions had been passed to the crew on the International Space-Station. Unaffected by the standing wave which blanketed the surface, they were able, after the twenty-four hours which they had been told to wait, to activate the space-borne defences which, even when everyone was talking about them, were still officially denied.

According to the most believable of rumours, it was a combination of nuclear warheads fired from Chinese and Russian satellites, plus lasers and more warheads from those of the USA which brought down the base-ship. The resultant feedback from the explosion was enough to cause all of the landed ships and all of the walkers to explode.

No-one could adequately explain just how such comparatively primitive weapons had been able to defeat the invaders, but some of the wilder rumours mentioned technology harvested from previous alien encounters. Nearly everyone mentioned Roswell. The governments of the world refused to either confirm or deny anything.

With the restoration of power and communications, civilization reasserted itself relatively quickly. The official death-toll was calculated at nearly 1 billion in the end. It would have been more, said the experts, but with so many military bases being located away from population centres, the plague did not have much chance to move out of rural areas and into the more densely-populated cities.

The world licked its wounds and considered itself lucky.

James returned to live on his parents' farm, and Bert sold his house and moved in with him. He was too old to find a new wife, he would say, but not too old to show a young man a thing or two.

Alan and Charlotte could not return to their pub, but with Andy and Sandra they bought out and renovated the derelict Outdoor Pursuits Centre, Dave, Dan and Daz did the refit.

Debbie, Ryan and Heidi were all just happy to get home

Nicola returned to her life and her job with a new lightness and optimism. She allowed Alyssa to play whatever she wanted in the car, especially as the girl seemed to have gone off Bohemian Rhapsody.

Tony did not return to his job, nor to any of the red-headed women from his past. Three weeks after the invasion, he and Nicola went out for dinner. Later they decided to mark the day of the invasion as their first date.

Acknowledgements

This book was originally written during NaNoWriMo 2011, something which I would never have undertaken – nor completed – without the encouragement and fellow-suffering of my wife, Kath, so immense thanks to her for that and so much more.

Thanks also to Elaine Borthwick who joined us on that month of intensive writing. It wouldn't have happened without you too.

Thanks also need to go to those who have read and commented on this book, and its cover. That means you, Daniel Carpenter, Jackie Summers, Cat Randle, Sarah Hilary, Simon Crump, Samuel Newcombe, Micheál Ó Coinn, Rachel Kendell, Cathy Bryant, Lorraine Harvey, Nettie Thomson, Susan Howe, Amanda Huggins, Sarah Logan, Sue Hornby, and Mike Harris.

Huge thanks should also go to all the various people who have helped and encouraged me in my writing over the years. You are far too numerous to mention, but you know who you are.

Finally, huge thanks to three more people, Mum and Dad – without whom none of this would ever have happened, and keep happening. – and, of course, H.G Wells.

Made in the USA
Charleston, SC
22 April 2013